LYDIA, WOMAN OF PURPLE

KIMBERLY BLACK

Steepledog Productions
Copyright © 2017 by Kimberly Black

Manufactured in the United States of America

ISBN: 1-946846-00-7
ISBN-13: 978-1-946846-00-6
Large Print ISBN: 978-1-946846-24-2

 Created with Vellum

DEDICATION

To my mother, Bobbie McLaughlin, who instilled in me a deep love for God's word and the joy of sharing it with others.

This book is a work of fiction, inspired by Lydia, a merchant of purple, mentioned in the Bible in the sixteenth chapter of Acts, as well as the believers who met in her home and were the recipients of the letter from the apostle Paul that makes up the book of Philippians. While the story is set in a real place, within the framework of real events, it is the product of my imagination. My hope is that my readers will be moved to seek out the message of love and encouragement found within the texts that inspired this novel.

Acknowledgments

My heartfelt appreciation to my friends, prayer partners, and beta readers (Ron, Beverly, Sally, Geni, and Kay) for your honesty, enthusiasm, and support. Endless love and thanks to Tammie Cleeton for standing alongside me as we teach another generation about God's infinite love. Thanks also to my dad and boss, Ken McLaughlin, for giving me the freedom to write whenever inspiration strikes.
I am especially grateful to my sons, Sam and Sean, and to my daughter-in-law, Whitney. Their limitless love recharges me when I'm exhausted and provides me with a true sense of home. Most of all, I wish to thank my husband, Riley, for the countless ways he loves, serves, sacrifices, and cares for me. Without him, I would never have finished this project.

A very special thanks to my artist son, Samuel Black, for the lovely cover art for this book.

CHAPTER
ONE

"They are coming! They are coming!"

Two little boys ran through the gates and into the colony of Philippi as the sun rose beyond the hills.

"They are almost here!" they shouted, announcing the early morning procession of travelers coming into the city on the Egnatian Way. The wide stone-paved road brought the merchants from the port at Neapolis directly into the agora, the market forum in the heart of the city.

Shopkeepers buzzed with anticipation as they awaited the arrival of their shipments from other ports off the Mediterranean Sea.

Lydia made room on her shelves for the new dyes and fabrics she expected today. Her booth was small—just twelve feet across and twice again as deep. The four cut-stone walls and flat roof were simple but adequate, with a narrow private door in the back and a wider opening in the front that was covered with a broad canvas awning. The market shops stood in three rows, forming a C-shape around an open courtyard where vendor carts and pallets held all kinds of foods and other products.

Lydia's location near the front northeast corner of the market square provided excellent visibility for travelers and convenient access for Philippian shoppers, as well.

She watched the boys race to join a group of children playing in the small stretch of grass in the market center while their parents prepared their shops. She smiled at their laughter, thinking back to her childhood days in Thyatira when she picked wild flowers as her parents prepared for their work.

"Are you expecting new merchandise?" Calchas asked, feigning a groan as he raised the awning on his own booth next to Lydia's.

"Yes." She motioned to the handsome youth leading the parade of merchants into town. "There is Marcus now." Her cousin led a donkey pulling a small cart loaded with crates. A girl sat on a container in the front of the wagon. "I wonder who she is."

"Ahh! That will be my treasure," Calchas said, a greedy grin spreading from ear to ear. "Ercole must have paid Marcus for the favor of a ride." He stroked the carefully curled silver whiskers that lined his lower jaw.

"Are you finally taking a wife?" Lydia asked her friend. As the cart rolled closer, she saw that the girl was just a child. "Or is she a relative?"

"We *bought* her," Calchas boasted. "Is she not lovely?"

Lydia saw a young girl, perhaps twelve, sitting on the

crates. She looked as thin as a sapling and had unusually fair skin and dark hair. The child wore a simple linen tunic with her hair covering pinned to the twisted braid at the back of her head. She crossed her arms around herself as if she were cold. Lydia wondered why a middle-aged idol merchant would purchase a frail-looking child slave. *Certainly not for a house servant*, Lydia thought.

Tall and muscular, Marcus easily maneuvered the donkey cart to the front of the idol shop and reached his hand up to the girl.

Calchas' younger partner, Ercole, hurried out to appraise his new acquisition. "Do not touch her!" Ercole shouted and batted Marcus's hand away. His gruff voice caused both Marcus and the girl to jump. Ercole took the girl's hand and stretched out her arm for Calchas' inspection.

The girl appeared frightened. Her petite frame shivered in the warm spring breeze. As Calchas circled the cart, Lydia took a step toward her and nodded. She hoped a friendly face would calm the child.

"Her name is Daphne." Ercole held fast to her hand, quickly establishing his dominance over the girl while still maintaining a sense of awe in her presence. "She is a seer, blessed by the Oracle of Delphi." He made a flourish with his left hand as he eased the girl down to the road with his right.

Lydia looked into Daphne's green eyes. Though Lydia had seen others with green eyes before, Daphne's pale gaze seemed unusual—detached and unfocused.

"Let us take her inside and allow her to rest," Ercole said. The two men and Daphne disappeared into Calchas' booth.

Marcus coaxed the donkey a few steps forward and

unloaded the crates into the shop as Lydia carried a basket of small jars inside.

"What is wrong with her?" Lydia asked Marcus in a hushed tone. "Was the journey so difficult, or is the girl ill?"

"She is not right, Lydia. She did not speak a word to me, and her hands shook when she was not holding fast to the cart. I think she must be frightened." He shrugged as he carried another carton of fabrics inside, and he said over his shoulder, "She is very young."

Lydia thought about her associates next door. She had known them for years, and though she hated the idol trade, she had always known them to be fair in their business practices and kind to their neighbors. "Ercole and Calchas can be stern, but they would never hurt her."

Marcus opened the first crate and emptied the rolls of fabric onto the center table, stacking them into a neat pyramid of dark blue linen. He opened the next carton while Lydia arranged the jars of dye on the shelves.

"I do not know what makes her fearful, but I believe it is neither Ercole nor Calchas. She reminds me of a temple sacrifice. It is like she sees things that are not there." Marcus finished stacking a second pyramid, this one of plum linen. "Do you believe she can see spirits, as Ercole says?"

"I know not about such things." Lydia sighed, wishing to avoid yet another conversation with her young cousin about the spirit world. "Ercole and Calchas sell their idols and amulets, telling their customers what they must do to please one god or another. I listen to them talk and wonder if they even believe the words they say. Always there is more for them to do. They never seem to run out of gods to worship with this favor or that charm."

"You believe in only one god," Marcus said with a laugh. "It is easier for you."

Lydia looked at her cousin as if she were considering the goods in her shop. Marcus was young—robust and sturdy. He easily unloaded the heaviest crates. Thick black curls crowned his bronzed head. His dark eyes contrasted with his gleaming white smile. He was smart, too. Lydia often enjoyed his sharp wit and natural humor, although others could be offended by it if they did not understand.

She thought back to when his mother died. Marcus was only eight years old and already as fierce as a lion. Having never known his father, Marcus had had to grow up fast and accept much adult responsibility while he was still a child. Lydia had promised her aunt to raise him as her own. She did her best but was never truly able to take the place of his mother.

She wished he believed in her God—her late husband's God. Jehovah was the source of her strength and comfort. Whenever she felt weak or lonely, she would pray or recite one of the many passages from scripture that Simeon had taught her. That was not enough for Marcus. Instead, he chased the favor of Apollo, Zeus, and Aphrodite, always searching for a new truth, greater power, and more love.

When he reached the age of seventeen and became a Roman citizen last month, Lydia prayed that God would soften his heart and call Marcus to Him. To Lydia's sorrow, when Marcus put away his childhood *bulla*, his small leather pouch of lucky amulets that he wore on a strap around his neck, he purchased several idols from Calchas and delved deeper into the study of the Olympians.

With all the crates emptied, Marcus took the donkey to the stable and Lydia remained alone in her booth. She arranged the new spools of linen thread in a large bowl on the center table. Sunlight filtered through the canvas awning on the front of her shop and made her fabrics glow with rich crimsons and purples.

"Elohai, my God, the soul You have breathed in me is pure. One day You will take it from me and restore it in the time to come. As long as it is within me, I will thank You," she prayed. "I thank You for Your protection of the merchants and their ships. I thank You for this beautiful morning You stretch out over us. I pray that all who enter my shop will see Your works and seek Your will."

Lydia closed her eyes and turned her face to the sun. She felt the warmth and remembered the way Simeon used to kiss her on both cheeks before they began each day. She imagined him next to her again and hoped that he was somehow listening to her prayer. She hoped someone heard her prayer. Just saying the words gave her a sense of something beyond this life. She took a deep breath and stepped into the agora courtyard, pulling her *epiblema*, her outer scarf, over her thick dark hair.

The other vendors opened their booths as well, and the local shoppers filled the forum.

"Lydia!" a shopkeeper called from across the court.

She waved and nodded. Two more people hailed her. She smiled at her neighbors and customers alike.

Nobody calls me Rachel anymore, she thought to herself.

Apart from Marcus, I do not believe another citizen in Philippi knows my real name.

Her Lydian accent was so prominent when she first arrived in the city years ago, that her friends and associates began to call her Lydia, and she eventually accepted the name as her own. Simeon, alone, called her Rachel until his death last year. She missed hearing her name, but she missed Simeon more.

A rise in the chatter around her caught her attention, and Lydia turned her head to see a group of four men entering the forum with travel packs over their shoulders. She had never seen them before. Though strangers were common in Philippi, the way these men strode into the city was unusually bold, almost as if they were expected. Everyone in the marketplace took notice.

Lydia saw that two wore basic tunics draped with shorter *himations*, or cloaks, and the other two men dressed in traditional Hebrew robes over their tunics, like what Simeon had worn.

"Two Greeks and two Jews—unlikely travel companions," she heard Calchas' graveled voice from behind her. He puffed up his rotund body and paced in front of his idol shop as if he was the authority on all religious traditions.

Never one to miss an opportunity for a sale, Ercole joined him and waved at the strangers. "Good travelers, welcome to our fine city. Come and see the wonders we offer. I would like to show you the amulets we have from the temple of Hermes, the god of safe travels. To keep away the evils and dangers of the road, eh?"

Lydia wondered if the men would accept his offer.

The leader of the foursome shook his nearly-bald head and smiled. "Our God, Jehovah, protects us. Thank you for your concern."

Lydia guessed he was the eldest of the four men.

She watched them make their way through the agora to the booths with fresh food. The men ate a small meal under a tree in the forum center court, gesturing to the city's architecture and to Mount Orbelos that stretched to the clouds just northeast of Philippi.

Shoppers bustled by, and Lydia smiled and nodded politely as she tended her booth. Several patrons perused her new merchandise. Lydia sold a dozen cuts of cloth and a small jar of her most expensive dye. When Marcus returned at midday, she rested and ate a quick meal of dried fish, cucumbers, and a little plum.

Afterward, she set herself the task of straightening her booth before the heavy afternoon traffic began. Marcus tended the entrance while she worked in the back. The warmth of the sun lifted the pungent aroma of the Tyrian purple dye. To those unaccustomed to the dyes, the odor could be overwhelming. Customers often coughed at the bitter smell, but it reminded Lydia of the countless afternoons on the Tyre seashore, working alongside her beloved Simeon, gathering mollusks for the dye.

Always aware of her customers' comfort, as soon as Lydia noticed the smell, she drew open the rear door of the booth which allowed a breeze to flow through.

Customers crowded the shop all afternoon, though most did not purchase. Lydia's merchandise consisted primarily of luxury items, and travelers seldom bought anything not necessary for their journeys. However, citizens from nearby towns as well as Neapolis knew the quality of her wares and often made the trip to buy her fabrics.

As the workday ended, Lydia watched the night prison guard relieve the day guard of his station. As Arsene, the night jailer, marched from the magistrate's office toward the jail, Lydia saw both citizens and centurions stepping out of his path. He stood at least a head taller than most men, and he wore a chiseled frown like other soldiers wore their helmets. Though Lydia considered Philippi a peaceful city, she understood the need for such men.

Looking across the agora, Lydia noticed that the four travelers were gone. She assumed they found a place to stay or moved on to the next town.

"Are you ready to go home?" she asked Marcus.

He stood at the entrance, but his thoughts wandered elsewhere.

Lydia asked again. "Marcus?" she finally said, putting her hand on his shoulder.

His attention returned. "Yes?"

"Where is your heart?" she asked. Simeon had often used this phrase when he caught her daydreaming.

"Will you be angry with me if I go see Daphne after we close the booth tonight?"

Lydia smiled. "Of course not. I think she would like a friend in a new place like this."

Marcus knit his dark brows and frowned at her answer. "I am not going to seek her friendship. I want her to see my future." His voice sounded short and annoyed to Lydia.

Her heart sank. She squeezed his hand and closed her eyes tightly in prayer.

"You are your own citizen, Marcus. I wish you would not seek the spirit world for answers, but how can I stop you?"

Marcus's face flushed red with indignation. He growled as he shouted. "You speak of my gods as if they are a child's game. They are real! I can see them. It is *your* god who is invisible."

Lydia did not expect his anger. Marcus often disagreed with her, but even then, he had always shown respect. This outburst had anger and resentment behind it, and it pierced her heart.

Marcus scowled and stomped away to talk to Ercole, leaving Lydia to take down her awning alone.

As she put everything away, she heard Calchas and Ercole bargaining with Marcus in the next booth. She closed her shop and sat on the small bench just outside the back door to wait.

Calchas' back door stood open, and she could see and hear everything. She thought about her own childhood when her mother had consulted a priestess about what to name her younger brother. She remembered the gnarled hands of the old prophetess as she cast bones onto a table. An icy shiver ran down Lydia's spine, and she decided to pray for Marcus's soul to be open to God's voice instead of Daphne's.

Daphne sat on a tall, slender stool, chewing on a leaf that Ercole handed her. Marcus faced her and stared intently into her eyes. Lydia recognized a mix of fear and excitement in his expression. Even in the lamplight, Lydia could see a bead of sweat forming above his lip.

Lydia took a deep breath, turned her face toward heaven, and then back to Marcus. She recited the prayer, just as Simeon taught her. "Blessed are You, Lord our God, King of the universe."

She watched Daphne take a sip from a bowl that Calchas gave her as Ercole fanned a lamp of incense. Calchas drank after her.

Lydia felt sick to her stomach and afraid for Marcus at the same time. She used the only weapon she knew. She prayed. "May it be Your will, oh Lord, to accustom us to Your ways." Lydia clutched her hands together in desperation.

Daphne began to rock back and forth, and a fountain of moans and unintelligible phrases poured from her lips.

"And do not lead us into the hands of sin," Lydia continued, "or into the hands of pride or perversity, nor into the hands of temptation or shame."

Calchas began to speak. "She says that you are a man of strength. Apollo watches over you and leads your ways."

Lydia watched as Marcus nodded and smiled. Her heart felt raw as she wrestled for her beloved boy in prayer.

Calchas continued as Daphne mumbled. "She sees trouble in your future, but by the hand of Zeus," he said, "you will overcome and be a mighty leader."

"And do not let the evil rule over us." Lydia finished. Peace swept through her heart, and she could no longer hear anything the others said. She stood up and began walking home. After a few seconds, Marcus caught up and kept pace at her side.

"Daphne saw my future." His voice carried a mixture of excitement and hesitation.

Lydia knew that Marcus was waiting for a reaction, but she only walked to her doorway without speaking a word.

"Is there something you wish to say to me?" Marcus asked as he followed his cousin inside their home. His words sounded like a challenge, and Lydia had no desire for any more confrontation.

She sighed. "Marcus, you and I were both raised with a multitude of gods and goddesses to worship. And we have both suffered great loss in our lives. The gods of Olympus brought me nothing but work. They never delivered me any solace when I was sad. They asked for rituals, tasks, and sacrifices. They demanded that I live up to a standard that they never matched. They were flawed and easily manipulated by each other. When I married Simeon, I embraced his God and found a better path. I found a perfect God of love and compassion. His laws were concrete, not shifting like sand. He is an unchanging foundation. When Simeon died, I found comfort in prayer. This I know. For me, it is a simple truth." She stared into his dark eyes, hoping to reach his heart.

Jehovah God, I am trying. I pray that You will help him to see You. If You are the Almighty, why will You not speak to him? Please?

She felt no inspired nudge. She heard no whisper. Her cousin made no response, so she continued, hoping for the right words to come. "I want you to know that you are my family and that I love you like you were my own son. That is also a fact." Lydia smiled. She felt a swell of confidence that her words touched him as she pulled back the covering from her hair. "There is nothing you can do that will ever change those truths."

Marcus chewed at his lip and clenched his fists. He snorted a fiery chuff and leaned down close to Lydia's face. "My gods may not have given me back my mother—not even a sufficient substitute—but yours did not give you back your husband, either. Those are the truths I know."

He stormed away into his room, leaving Lydia alone, fighting back tears. *Oh, God, my own faith is too weak. How will I ever persuade him?*

After a fitful night with little sleep, Lydia struggled to keep her mind focused. She cleaned and straightened her booth, as usual, greeted her customers and made several sales, but her heart lingered on Marcus. She still felt unsettled by his outburst and by his infatuation with the Greek gods. *If Simeon were here, he would know what to say,* she thought. Her husband's faith had been strong. *Strong enough for both of us.*

Lydia nodded to Ercole, who stood at the post between his booth and hers. He tended his shop while Calchas paraded Daphne around the forum, announcing to everyone within reach of his voice that Philippi was now graced with its own seer. To promote his new asset, he gave all takers a small token of a copper ring formed in the shape of a python, one of the many symbols of Apollo.

People chattered about how young and beautiful the new seer was. Calchas bragged that Daphne's youth and purity ensured accurate readings from the spirit world. Daphne smiled and nodded to the crowds but never appeared impressed or awed by anything. As Calchas returned the girl to their booth, Ercole received the new clients and their money.

Lydia watched the line form and stretch across her shop entrance. Several patrons browsed through her linens while waiting for their turn with Daphne. For a moment, Lydia thought about the fortune she might make with Daphne next door. Though she disapproved of his products, Lydia admired Calchas' shrewdness in business. *For the price of a few tiny copper rings, Calchas collects a pouch full of silver coins.* She shook her head and banished those thoughts. *And at what cost for his customers?*

At mid-day, Marcus arrived, and Lydia rested for a moment to eat. She returned to find her cousin cheering the crowds in line to visit Daphne. He told them about his reading from the previous day. He invited them into Lydia's booth to find the perfect fabrics and ornaments to adorn their charms and idols.

Lydia called him inside. She kept to the business at hand, hoping his anger from the night before had cooled.

"Marcus, I know that you wish to take advantage of the crowds, but we must tend to our own business and allow Ercole to take care of himself."

He frowned. "What do you suppose I am doing?" He spoke with urgency. "These people are ripe for plucking."

Lydia's heart pounded with conviction. Marcus's words reflected her own selfish thoughts from just moments earlier. She took a deep breath, and the musky aroma of purple filled her lungs, calming her. She restrained her voice, and in a firm, quiet tone said, "I understand that you want our business to be profitable. However, we must remember that these people are our friends and our customers. They are not olives to be plucked and pressed."

She smiled at a patron admiring a spool of crimson cording. Lydia tilted her head to further soften her stance with Marcus. "You are a good salesman. That is one of your many strengths. You need not rely on Ercole or Calchas to provide us with patrons."

Marcus's frustration appeared to melt with her compliments. Lydia patted him on the shoulder. "Come inside from the sun's heat and attend to our own customers." She gestured to the woman at the spools.

He nodded and approached the well-dressed customer. "Ah, you have good taste," he said. "We received this only yesterday. It came directly from Tyre."

Marcus escorted the client around the shop and, within twenty minutes, helped her to purchase the cording and two cuts of fabric. Lydia smiled her approval from across the booth.

As she watched Marcus work with customers, her concerns about him dimmed. His confident voice greeted patrons like old friends. His knowledge about the products impressed them. His eagerness attracted new shoppers. *If only he knew how proud I am.*

Lydia remembered the day she helped her aunt give birth to Marcus. He was a big, healthy baby and grew into a tall, stubborn young man. His mother often complained that his pig-headedness caused too much strife, but Lydia suggested that his steadfastness could be a great asset for a businessman.

Watching him now, she felt he proved her right. She wished her aunt had lived to see Marcus grown.

Lydia noticed a crowd gathering in the center courtyard. One of the Jewish men from the previous day stood in the midst of the assembly, talking. She wondered if he was a traveling peddler. She heard his voice over the people's murmurs but could make out only a few words.

"The Messiah has come," she heard him say. As quickly as she understood the phrase, the surrounding crowd hummed excitedly, drowning out his voice.

She stepped out of her booth to hear more, but after a few minutes, the men moved to the road and north to the theater, out of sight. She looked to the mountaintops, where heavy gray clouds formed and rolled toward the city. A cool breeze swept through Philippi, and she retreated to her booth.

Marcus stood at the lamp with the censer. He placed a mixture of herbs into the incense cup and used the lamp to set them burning.

"I thought we might need this to keep the shop smelling sweet for the customers when the rain begins." He moved the censer to the middle of the booth.

Lydia smiled and nodded. Once the rain started, the shoppers deserted the forum, and the shopkeepers spent the afternoon cleaning and organizing their goods. Lydia started at the back and inventoried her dyes.

Her thoughts tarried on the word *Messiah*. She remembered the gleam in Simeon's eyes when he spoke of the coming Messiah, the savior, and king of the Jews. He spent hours telling Lydia about how things would change when the Messiah came. The prophets had spoken at length of the Savior who would come and take his place on the throne of David, bringing a sacrifice of forgiveness and the resurrection with him.

Though Lydia never actually understood all that Simeon talked about, she never forgot his words. "I have faith in my God, and He will not disappoint me."

She thought back to her grandmother and namesake, Rachel, who was also Jewish. She remembered asking her about why she only believed in one God when the rest of the family served many. "My sweet child, if you serve the God who creates the world and the heavens, why would you need any other?" She would invariably smile then, creating a twinkle in her eyes, and add, "We pray to The One who made the stones and metals from which all the other gods are cast."

Lydia tried to smile through the memories, but now a painful pounding in her head pushed the pleasant thoughts away.

Her stomach churned. Her eyes stung at the corners, and she had difficulty focusing. She sat down for a moment and searched the room for Marcus. He sat on a stool next to the censer, inhaling deeply. His body swayed slightly.

"Is this my regular incense?" Lydia asked. Her words boomed in her own head.

"No." Marcus's voice cut sharply.

Lydia's heartbeat pounded loudly in her ears, and she clutched her stomach. "Where did you get it?"

"Calchas gave it to me." His words sounded raspy and detached.

Lydia pulled off her hair covering and put her clammy fingers to the back of her neck. It felt hot to the touch. The sound of rain on the roof rose to a roar. Lydia struggled for air, and when she finally managed a deep breath, it burned her lungs.

She stood, and the room seemed darker. She staggered to the back door, still trying to focus her eyes. She stepped into the sheeting rain and fell to her knees, retching over the bench. Her stomach cramped, and she vomited into the bin of garbage behind the shops.

The rain cooled her body and cleared her head. She sat and shivered for several minutes on her bench, concentrating on slow, steady breaths. She tried praying, but her thoughts wandered, and anger clouded her heart.

Not only had Calchas and Ercole's business poisoned her cousin's mind, now their concoctions poisoned her body, as well.

When she felt solid on her feet, she marched back into the shop and snatched the censer from its stand. She spun around quickly and carried it outside where the heavy rain extinguished the smoldering herbs.

Marcus stumbled after her. When he saw the water wash away his mixture of leaves and resins, he roared, "Those are not yours!"

Lydia turned to face her cousin. The wild look in his dark eyes startled her. He began waving his arms fiercely. She stepped away but not soon enough to avoid the back of his hand. He did not hit her hard, but her footing was unstable in the mud, and she fell in a heap.

Marcus bent down and grabbed the brass bowl from the mud and turned away from Lydia, disappearing into the storm.

THREE

Lydia closed her booth alone and waited for the storm to pass. Within an hour, the dark clouds retreated beyond the mountains and the skies cleared. The puddles drained quickly, and her path home waited. Every step she took brought new trouble to mind.

What has happened to Marcus? Why has he suddenly grown so steadfast in his devotion to Apollo? A few months ago, he cared little for his charms and idols. She wondered if he would be home when she arrived. She let her mind drift to what might have been. *If only Simeon had not become sick, things would be better between Marcus and her.* Perhaps Marcus spent time with Calchas and Ercole because he needed a father figure. She prayed for wisdom.

Agatha, Lydia's maidservant, was waiting for her at her door. "Why are you alone? Where is Marcus?" she asked.

Lydia looked at Agatha with kindness, seeing only compassion and concern in her dark eyes. Though she was only a few months older than Lydia, Agatha filled the role of caretaker with listening ears and soft, rounded shoulders to lean upon. She helped Lydia remove her still-damp epiblema and waited for an answer.

"Marcus and I argued. I hoped he was already here."

"Oh Mistress, your cheek is red and swollen. What happened?" Agatha widened her eyes as she examined Lydia's face. A look of hurt and anger settled in her expression as she realized what made the bruise on her mistress's cheek. "Did he strike you?"

Lydia dismissed the question with a wave of her hand. "I am fine. It was an accident. I need to prepare for Shabbat supper. I must change."

Agatha followed Lydia to her room and helped her into a clean tunic. She combed through Lydia's thick black curls and twisted her hair into a tight roll against her head. She used a brass pin with a jade bead to secure Lydia's purple epiblema over her hair.

Agatha studied Lydia's expression and finally said, "This mark on your face is quite noticeable. Shall I bring some of your powder to cover it?"

"I will do it." Lydia took her small jar of crushed pearls and dipped her brush in the powder. Sweeping the dust over her cheeks, she winced at the pain she felt at even the lightest touch. She found herself wanting to hit something... anything.

"Are you ready, Mistress?" Agatha waited at the door.

Lydia examined her face in the polished silver hand mirror and nodded. "I am."

The two women went downstairs to the low dining table

and took their places for supper. Though the household servants worked tirelessly throughout the day to prepare for the special meal, Lydia insisted that they join her for the Sabbath meal and prayers.

Phoebe, who worked in the kitchen, carried in the last water pitcher and the table was ready. Her husband, Joel, and their nine-year-old twins, Eb and Mary, joined them, sitting on cushions around the table. The only missing member of Lydia's household was her young cousin.

"Where is Marcus?" Eb asked. "Will we wait for him?"

The others looked to Lydia for an answer. She dipped her chin and shook her head. "No," she said, just above a whisper. "I do not believe Marcus will join us tonight."

Lydia lit the candles and recited the blessing for the holy day as everyone allowed their shoulders to relax. Through the west-facing archway, Lydia watched the sun settle behind the hills. The Sabbath had begun.

The family started the meal with prayers over the wine and *challah*, traditional egg bread, and then proceeded to the lamb and lentil stew. Lydia tried to calm her thoughts, but her mind lingered on Marcus's temper.

As she looked around the table, she saw Agatha's round smile, Eb and Mary's bright young faces, and the shared, knowing glances between Joel and Phoebe. She missed Marcus. She missed Simeon. She drifted on a salty sea of wishes and memories when something Eb said pulled her to the present.

"What does *Messiah* mean?" he asked.

Lydia focused on the boy's face, glowing in the candlelight. "It means Savior," she answered automatically.

"Yes," Joel agreed with a nod. "I remember the master speaking of the coming Messiah. He will be a king to the Jews and will bring atonement."

Eb's dark eyes glistened with excitement. "What is atonement, Father?"

"It means he will bring a perfect sacrifice in payment for the sins of God's children. Our sins will be forgiven, not just rolled back for a time." Joel looked to Lydia for approval. She dipped her chin and smiled.

"Are we God's children, Father?" Mary asked.

"Yes, dear one," Joel answered. "Even though we are Greek, we have adopted the faith of our master in the one true God." Joel reached out and cupped his daughter's face in his hands, and Phoebe patted her son's shoulder.

Agatha released a sweet sigh and took another sip of her wine. "Such a beautiful evening,"

Lydia almost ignored her. "Eb, why did you ask about the Messiah?"

"When I was in the market this morning, buying barley for Mother, I heard a man talk about the Messiah," Eb explained.

"What did he say?" Lydia felt a strange curiosity growing inside of her, and for a moment her worries of Marcus disappeared.

Eb sat up straight, stretching as tall as he could while seated. He spread an important grin across his lips. "The man said," he began, speaking clearly to his mistress, "that he had seen the Messiah. He said that he was killed but was alive again."

"Pshaw," Joel scoffed. "Another story of a sorcerer doing tricks. I hear about these magicians all the time."

Phoebe clicked her tongue at her son. "Eb, you cannot always believe the things you hear in the market. Everybody there is selling something."

"Yes, mother," Eb said, his shoulders sinking in disappointment.

"Do not look so downcast," Agatha said, always encouraging. "When the true Messiah comes, we will hear and be sure."

Mary chirped, "You never know, Eb, maybe he will come tomorrow."

As the dinner ended with the blessings of thanksgiving, Lydia kissed every member of her household on each cheek and then wandered out to her portico to pray. Her prayers were short, as thoughts of the day mingled with her requests and praise.

She searched the darkness for Marcus but saw nothing. She listened for his voice but heard only the night wind in the trees. A shiver raced down her spine, and she raised her gaze to the stars. "Oh, God of creation," she said.

"May I do anything for you, Mistress?" Agatha asked from the doorway.

Lydia's smile welled up from her soul as she faced her friend and reached with both hands. "Yes, Agatha, come sit with me a while."

The two women met at the bench to the side of the door and sat side-by-side. Lydia studied Agatha's face and noticed a few new wrinkles at the corners of her eyes. She saw the hints of silver at her friend's temples and raised her hand to her own face. Agatha had been Lydia's maidservant since they were both sixteen years old. Twenty years of devotion had made the two women inseparable. Lydia trusted Agatha with her home, and Agatha trusted Lydia with her life.

"Have we grown into our mothers?" Lydia asked. She remembered the day they first met, only a week before her wedding to Simeon. Agatha had been her constant companion ever since.

"Do not worry about Marcus.," Agatha squeezed her hand. "He is grown. He can manage himself."

Lydia nodded and moved her finger to her bruised cheek. She winced at the lingering pain. "I cannot help but be concerned. If he is violent today, what kind of a man will he be tomorrow?"

"He does not appreciate you as a mother," Agatha added. "Give him time. He is young. We were young once." She laughed.

Lydia smiled. She could always depend on Agatha to give her a different perspective on her problems. She leaned back against the wall. "Oh, Agatha, do you think it is even possible?" Her mind wandered ahead of her words.

"Is what possible? That we were young? What are you asking?"

Lydia laughed at her disconnected question. "You must forgive me, friend. My thoughts skip like a stone across water." She took Agatha's hand. "Do you think it possible that the Messiah has come?"

Agatha shrugged, and Lydia sensed pity in her expression. "I could not say," Agatha began. "If there was a new king, would we not know? If the Messiah were here, then I would think that God would want the whole world to know."

Lydia's heart sank. Though Agatha always had a cheerful temperament, Lydia knew that she was reasonable and honest and never raised unrealistic hopes.

As Lydia's expression wilted, Agatha added, "Why not pray for an open heart? You often suggest that very thing when I am troubled."

Lydia nodded, still deflated, and rose to her feet to allow Agatha to go back into the house. As Lydia stepped out from the cover of the portico, she looked to the heavens. "Lord God, Creator of the Universe, grant me…" She paused as a breeze brought a quick shower of raindrops from the nearby leaves down to her face.

The cold droplets startled her and sent shivers dancing down her back. The fine hair on her arms stood on end, and she blinked in dismay. As she retreated into her home, she whispered one more request. "Lord God, I ask only for wisdom to know Your truth."

As soon as the words left her lips, she wondered why she had asked for that. After all the troubles she had seen these last few days, she feared what the truth might bring.

CHAPTER

FOUR

Lydia and Agatha rose early the next morning to meet with the small group of Jewish believers for prayers, as they did each week. They followed the path through the olive grove to the river beyond the city's eastern gate. The usual meeting place was a small clearing where the river bent around a rocky outcropping, causing the waters to move more slowly.

Agatha often commented that though she had never visited a synagogue before, she could not imagine anywhere more tranquil than this place of prayer. There were fewer than ten Hebrew men in Philippi, which was the minimum requirement for the presence of a synagogue, so the believers of Jehovah worshiped together at the river's edge.

"Shalom." Clement greeted the women with his usual blessing of peace. The elderly man nodded to Lydia as she took her seat on the rocks. Agatha sat next to her on a lower rock.

"Shalom," Lydia replied, squeezing Agatha's hand.

Soon two more women arrived. Syntyche and Euodia greeted the others with smiles and blessings and quickly found their seats. Euodia's maidservant followed them and perched on a rock at her mistress's feet.

The small gathering waited quietly for three more people to arrive. Two older women and a young girl joined the group. The sound of the wind rustling through the shade trees' leaves harmonized with the gentle song of the river. Clement stood and began to recite from the Psalms.

As Clement's fragile voice spoke the ancient Hebrew verses of King David's lament, Lydia's eyes burned with tears. She listened to the words. She understood David's feeling of desolation, as though God had turned His face away. She wanted to cry out as David did. She wished for healing. She prayed that God would mend the rift with her cousin. She prayed for restoration. She prayed for…

"A psalm of David?" a stranger's voice asked.

Lydia turned her head to see who spoke.

The four strangers from the market appeared and greeted the group.

"Welcome to you," Clement said, gesturing for the men to join their worship. "We have no synagogue in Philippi, so we invite Jehovah outdoors. You may celebrate the Sabbath with us if you wish."

"May the blessings of the Lord be upon you, and thank you for your welcome," their leader said. "I am Paul of Tarsus, and these are my friends, Silas, Timothy, and Luke." He nodded to each one as they sat among the others.

Lydia shifted closer to Agatha to make room for another.

The youngest of the four men, Timothy, sat next to her. She smiled and nodded, guessing that he was only a year or two older than Marcus.

Clement continued with his reading. "Save your people and bless your inheritance; be their shepherd and carry them forever."

"Do you believe that God will send a Messiah?" Paul asked when Clement paused.

Lydia's ears perked up, and she watched carefully. Clement stood as tall as his bent frame could extend. He faced the stranger's question with strength. "Sir, we constantly pray that the Lord will speak again and send a leader to save His people."

Lydia and the others nodded in agreement. She wondered if this man, Paul, intended to challenge Clement's knowledge.

Paul stood and softened his voice. "I, too, prayed for God's favor. I was impatient and felt that God remained silent for too long. I spent years studying the Holy Words so that I would know the Messiah if I saw Him."

Silas rose and patted his friend's shoulder.

Lydia noticed the encouragement Silas' presence gave Paul. She felt her heart pound in her chest. These men intrigued her.

"I expected a king on a throne. I expected governments to topple. I expected the Jewish leaders to be elevated to governors. I expected earthly power," Paul explained.

Lydia swallowed hard. Simeon had said similar things about the anticipated Messiah over and over. She wished that Simeon were with her now. He would have loved to hear this man speak.

"What I failed to see was that man's power is not God's power. The plans of men are small compared to the plan of God." Paul smoothed his hands over his robes and continued. "To my sorrow and shame, I did not know the Savior when He came. I did not know His message. It was not what I expected it to be. It was not what I wanted it to be."

Paul formed his hands into tight fists. "I expected a kind of revolution. I thought the Messiah would claim a throne and declare God's people the ruling class. Instead, His message was that of love and compassion for sinners. He exalted the lowly and humbled the haughty." Paul dropped his head until his chin almost touched his chest. His tone turned solemn. "In my pride and self-righteousness, I sought to destroy His followers. And with many ... I succeeded."

Clement blinked and began to shake. Lydia's heart beat faster. Her palms became moist, and her fingertips throbbed. She listened carefully, struggling to understand Paul's message. He was explaining his own personal experience with a savior. *How can that be?*

Clement took a step toward Paul. "Are you saying that the Messiah has come?"

"I have seen Him, myself," Paul said.

The whole gathering gasped. Lydia studied the faces of the three men who had come with Paul. They nodded. She could see that, to them, this was not a show or spectacle—it was a simple truth.

"Where is He? What is His name?" Clement asked. His voice sounded hoarse and strained. Lydia could not tell if he was skeptical or desperate. She was not certain of her own feelings, either.

"His name is Jesus, a man of Nazareth," Paul began. He spent the next hour telling them all about Jesus' work and teaching. Paul explained about his own experience with Jesus. He told of how he had been approached by Jesus on his way to Damascus—how he was blinded and then healed.

Lydia listened intently. Paul and Silas both explained how Jesus had come to save not only the Jews but everyone. They described in detail Jesus' trial, crucifixion, and resurrection. Paul talked about Jesus' return to Heaven. Silas told the group of Paul's dream that led them to Philippi.

Luke, the older of the two Greek men, finally spoke. "My friends tell you the truth. Jesus of Nazareth is the Messiah for whom we have all waited. He is the Son of Jehovah."

Lydia's mind no longer seemed cluttered with worry. She felt strong. She felt as though God spoke directly to her—as though He had listened to all the worries of her heart, and answered each one with a single name. Before she knew it, she was standing before Paul with her hands opened upward in submission.

"I want to be baptized as you were," she said. "I believe that Jesus of Nazareth *is* the Messiah and Son of God." She felt the stares of the others on her back, but she did not care. For the first time in over a year, she experienced pure peace.

Paul took her aside and listened to her as she poured out her heart's troubles in confession and dedication. When she turned back, she saw Agatha, Clement, and the others also asking Paul to baptize them.

Lydia pulled the pin from her hair and folded her

epiblema carefully, placing it on the rocks. She followed Paul into the cold Gangitis River. His strong hands held hers, and he prayed over her. He lowered her body into the river. She felt the icy water close all around her and let go of the fear and pain to which she had clung for years, and it seemed to drift away in the current. She felt the warm grip of Paul's arm pulling her up from the river. She could breathe again. *She could breathe again.*

Silas stood at the bank to help her out of the water, and Timothy and Luke warmed her with their extra robes. Lydia wrapped her purple scarf back around her hair and shoulders. Her body trembled as she sat on the rocks, waiting for the others, but she did not know if the shaking was from the cold or from the excitement she felt.

In the quiet moments, before the others returned to the rocks, she remembered Simeon. She thanked God for him. She felt grateful that he had shared his faith with her. It was this faith that brought her to this meeting and to this decision.

The sun rose high overhead as Paul and Syntyche climbed up from the water and into the waiting arms of Silas and Timothy. Everyone shivered and smiled. Luke, who was a doctor, suggested that the group get inside a warm house soon. Clement agreed and wished his friends a good Shabbat. Syntyche, Euodia, and the others hugged Lydia and Agatha and then left hurriedly for home. The four men appeared joyful as they pulled their damp robes over their tunics.

Agatha tugged at Lydia's sleeve. "We should get home quickly, too, Mistress."

Lydia thought about her home and its many empty rooms. She thought about what Simeon would have done had he been with her today. "Just a moment, Agatha," Lydia said with a nod. She turned to the men. "May I ask where you are staying in Philippi?"

Silas faced her and smiled. "We have a room at the inn near the west gate."

"Oh no," Lydia said, shaking her head. "That is too far from the agora and the town's center. You will spend half your day walking back and forth. My home is near the forum. You will all come and stay with me."

Paul laughed. "That is kind of you, but there are four of us. It would be an imposition."

"My house is large," she explained. "I have plenty of room." She did not want to sound proud or overbearing, but she simply *knew* they must come with her. She needed to hear more. Her whole family needed their message. *Marcus needed their message.*

"You are a generous woman, we have no doubt, but it would be best for us to stay at the inn," Timothy said. His youth and independence reminded Lydia of Marcus.

"Nonsense," she insisted. "If you consider me a believer in Jesus and His Way, then you will come and stay at my house." Lydia raised her eyebrows and waited for their reply.

Paul laughed and nodded. "Yes, my friends, I believe the Lord has a firm hold of her heart." He picked up his bag and slung it over his shoulder. The other men did the same. "We will follow you."

"Thank you." Lydia lead them toward the city gate. "You will honor my house."

Lydia's house servants greeted them at the door.

"You are all wet," Joel said, sending Eb back inside for blankets. "Did it rain again?"

Lydia helped Eb and Joel hand out blankets to Paul and Silas. She gave one to Agatha and took one for herself. "You will be wet, too, before the day is over," she said cheerfully. "These men bring good news."

Lydia introduced the four men to her household staff. They welcomed the travelers and took their things to the large receiving room on the first floor. Agatha went right to the kitchen to serve the meal.

They all reclined around the low table to eat, and Paul recounted his experiences to the others after the traditional prayers.

"Thanks be to God that the Messiah *has* come," Joel said, finishing his stew. "He turned to Eb and patted his shoulder. "Just as you said, Eb."

"Will you be baptized as well?" Lydia asked.

Eb jumped to his feet. "I drew plenty of water yesterday. The trough is full."

Lydia and her household went out to the stable, and Joel, Phoebe, Eb, and Mary asked Paul to baptize them.

Once they were all back inside and dry again, Lydia showed her new friends their rooms. She instructed Joel and Eb to make them comfortable. The guests spent the evening talking to their hosts about Jesus' life and message. The four men offered their individual stories over dinner, and the more they shared, the stronger Lydia felt. After the meal, Silas began a short song of blessing that filled the house.

When he finished, Phoebe and Mary cleared the table,

and the men went out to the courtyard for more conversation. Eb was anxious to tell the guests that he was the first to mention them to his family.

As she did each evening, Lydia went to her portico to pray. She thanked God for sending His messengers to Philippi. She prayed for the town to receive the good news. She prayed for Marcus's heart to be opened. She prayed for God to move Ercole and Calchas away from their city and to take away their influence.

"Mistress?" Phoebe said, touching Lydia's bent shoulder. "I am sorry to interrupt you, but is there anything else you need before bed?"

"Just one thing, Phoebe," Lydia said as she rose and went inside. "Is Marcus here?"

"I did not see him come in, but there is a lamp burning in his room. He has not said a word to anyone today. Is he ill?"

"No, I do not think so." Lydia squeezed Phoebe's hand. "Thank you."

Phoebe nodded and excused herself.

Lydia started up the stairs to her room.

"Before you retire," Luke said, stopping her on the second step. "I have something for you."

Lydia turned to face her guest. "Something for me?" She walked back down the steps and raised her gaze to meet his. Luke was tall and slim, with broad shoulders and a smooth jaw. She supposed him to be a few years older than herself, perhaps forty.

"I noticed that you had an injury on the side of your face." His voice was gentle. "I helped Phoebe make this poultice for you. Dab it over the redness before you sleep. In the morning, the swelling should be down."

He held the bowl of paste where she could see its contents.

"It smells sweet," Lydia said, inhaling the aroma of the spicy mixture.

"Honey, raisins, and herbs," Luke said. "It tastes good, too."

"Thank you." She took the bowl. "Thank you for everything."

Luke nodded and went to his room for the night.

Lydia looked down the long corridor to Marcus's bedroom. A pale glow shone around the edges of his door. She wanted to go and talk to him, but something in her heart told her to go to bed. She offered one more prayer for Marcus.

As she smoothed the pasty concoction over her cheek, she felt her face pulse and tingle. The muscle began to ache. She covered the sticky mixture with a small piece of cloth and went to bed.

Her eyes resisted closing. The excitement of the day mixed with ideas of how to tell Marcus what happened. As she tried to plan what to say, her thoughts wandered to Simeon. She knew he would be happy for her. She wished...

She stared out her window at the stars. They sparkled like jewels on a vast field of deep purple. *Such a color*, she thought. *The color of kings.*

FIVE

"The swelling is almost gone." Luke examined Lydia's face. His dark eyes narrowed as he nodded his approval. "You heal quickly."

"Thank you for your kindness. And your skill." Lydia dipped her chin in thanks.

Paul smiled and broke a piece of bread from the small loaf in front of him. He saluted her. "We are grateful for your hospitality." He said, dropping the bite into his mouth. "The comfort of your home surpasses any inn."

Silas hummed and turned his face to the morning sunlight that poured through the open arch facing east. Agatha placed another bowl of dates on the table.

"Have you seen Marcus this morning, Agatha?" Lydia asked. "Marcus is my young cousin," she explained to the men. "I suppose he was keeping to himself yesterday."

"I have not," Agatha answered. "I will ask Joel to see to him."

"Thank you, Agatha."

Luke watched as Lydia and Agatha exchanged glances. He regarded Timothy. "Young men can be impulsive. Especially when they have strong wills."

Timothy grinned sheepishly. "We depend on older and wiser men for guidance."

"We all struggle with temperaments," Paul said. "One person's weakness amplifies another's strengths."

"This is true," Silas agreed. He took another date from the bowl and smiled. "A morning like this should fill all of us with overflowing joy."

Luke and Timothy laughed. "Our friend, Silas, has never known a bad day," Timothy remarked.

Silas leaned back with a deep belly laugh. "Who has time for bad days?" he asked his young friend. "I have too many people to talk to. Too many friends to make."

Lydia smiled at the man's enthusiasm. "Where have you traveled with your news?"

Paul began listing city after city from Jerusalem to Antioch and from Tarsus through Phrygia.

"Almost as far west as Lydia?" she asked.

Paul and Silas both nodded. "Do you have family there?" Silas asked.

"My husband's family is still in Tyre. My family is from Thyatira. Have you been there?" she asked, hoping for news from the area.

Paul shook his head. "Not yet. I had hoped to go through that territory, but the Spirit stopped us."

"What do you mean?" Agatha asked. "What spirit?"

"The Holy Spirit of God—it is in you now—it seals the

hearts of believers. It guides your steps in God's will," Silas explained.

Paul told them of how the Spirit had prevented them from going northward into Bithynia and instead directed them to Philippi. "We had a vision of a Man of Macedonia crying out for us. When we arrived, we found a group of women in prayer—and your friend Clement, as well."

"I hope we were not a disappointment to you," Agatha said with a sly chuckle.

Luke smiled. "In my life, I have been granted the privilege of knowing many great women. I even have had the honor of speaking with Mary, the mother of Jesus. It was not difficult to see why God selected her among all women. Jesus knew many women who traveled with and provided for Him and His apostles. These women are some of the most devoted and faithful followers I have ever seen. These last two days have only increased that number." Luke faced Agatha and Lydia with a guileless look. He smiled and said, "Especially you."

Timothy raised his cup to salute Agatha and Lydia. "I would agree. We all feel quite at home because of your kindness and hospitality."

"This is a sight!" Marcus said in an agitated voice. "My own table is surrounded by strangers."

As Lydia jumped to her feet, Marcus spun around and stomped toward the door.

"Please, Marcus, come back and meet our friends," she pleaded.

"Your friends are not my friends, cousin." He shouted loud enough for everyone in the house to hear.

"Marcus, what is wrong?" Lydia asked.

"You seem to care more for strangers than for your relatives." Marcus continued marching to the door.

Lydia followed him out to the small portico. "Marcus, stop!"

He twisted at the waist to face her, shooting an angered expression her way. "I am a grown man, and I can come and go as I please." He straightened his shoulders and walked away toward the market. "You should be on your way to open your booth," he spat over his shoulder.

Lydia watched as Marcus stormed away. Tears flooded her eyes faster than she could wipe them away. She drew several deep breaths to clear her mind before she went back into the house.

Everyone was standing, waiting for her return.

"I apologize for my cousin's rudeness," she said.

Agatha shook her head and clutched her hands to her chest. "He is just ..."

Paul held up a calming hand. "Do not trouble yourself. We understand. We have all raised our voices in anger against people who did nothing to deserve it."

Lydia fixed a weak smile on her lips and nodded. "I should be on my way to my booth, though." She gestured to Agatha. "Please make sure that our guests have whatever they need."

Agatha nodded and began to clear the table.

Paul smiled at his host. "Perhaps we should go back to the inn tonight."

Silas agreed. "We should. And we need to find a good place for a group to assemble."

Lydia was about to leave when she heard their exchange. "You all will stay right here. We have plenty of room for a large gathering. Eb and Joel can draw as much water as you need. Please do not go back to the inn because of Marcus."

Luke offered a reassuring smile. "We will stay for the night, but if we are going to establish a church in Philippi, we will need a permanent meeting place."

Lydia blinked and laughed. "Everyone in this town knows my house. You will not find a better place."

Paul shook his head again. "This will be too much for one household. The meetings will be every day for a while. They may stretch into the night. People will be hungry at times. You are a generous woman, but this would be a long-term commitment."

"And how long do you intend to tell people about Jesus?" she asked him. Her tone was unapologetic.

As Paul paused, Lydia placed her hands on her hips, waiting for a response.

Luke began to snicker. Timothy and Silas both raised their eyebrows, anticipating his answer.

Paul swallowed. "I intend to speak the good news of Jesus with my dying breath."

"I expected that to be the case," Lydia said. She employed the tone she reserved for bartering in her shop. "And do you think that I will grow tired of having fellow-believers in my home? That I will grow weary of the name of the Messiah?"

Luke's shoulders shook as he tried to restrain his laughter. "Paul, brother, I think you lost this argument. You should surrender with grace."

Paul shrugged, sighed, looked at Lydia for a long

moment, and considered. "I suppose," he said delicately, "we have found our place of worship."

Satisfied with the announcement, and the outcome, Lydia left her home for the agora.

She walked her usual route, but this morning felt different. For the first time since Simeon had passed, she had a sense of purpose and direction. She no longer felt as though she was in Philippi only because it was a good situation for her husband's business. She now believed that God needed her here to increase His kingdom. The confrontation with Marcus troubled her, but at the same time, she knew that God would provide her with the right words to soften him and guide him to Jesus.

A warm breeze danced through the branches of the trees, and a refreshing chill ran down Lydia's spine. Excitement and expectation fluttered in her mind as she thought of all the people who would soon gather at her home.

She knew her friends from the riverside prayer meetings would be there, and she wondered if the travelers would bring many others.

When she arrived at her booth, the front awning was up, and Marcus was in the back, polishing the bottles of dye. Lydia fixed a smile to her face and softened her shoulders. "Good morning, Marcus."

He acknowledged her with a placid expression. He moved from cleaning the bottles of dye to the spools of thread. "I am no longer a child, Lydia." His tone was calm.

"I know that, Marcus. I did not intend to treat you as a child," she replied. "I know that you are a responsible young man. You are capable of making your own decisions."

Marcus squared his shoulders, standing as tall as he could manage without obviously stretching. His thick, dark hair and tanned complexion seemed to be lit from within. "I appreciate all that you have sacrificed to care for me over the years. I... apologize for my lack of manners with your friends."

Lydia understood how difficult it was for him to utter the words. She tilted her head and looked into his eyes. "Thank you, Marcus. You are dear to me." She patted his arm and smiled. She took the dusting cloth from his hands. "I will finish this. You should stand up front and watch for new customers."

Marcus strode to the front of the shop and faced the morning sun. "This afternoon I plan to visit the palaestra. Some of my friends have challenged me to wrestle. They say that working in this shop has made me soft. I will show them the strength of Apollo." He laughed as if he expected Lydia to join him in the joke.

She just nodded and allowed a silent prayer to fill her brain.

"How long do you expect your friends to stay here in Philippi?" he asked.

Before Lydia could answer, a customer entered the shop, and Marcus attended to their needs.

Lydia took another moment of prayer, perhaps more of a wish, to ask for Paul and his friends to stay in Philippi long enough to win Marcus over to Jesus.

By the time the customer left with his purchase, Marcus seemed to have forgotten his question. The market began to bustle with shoppers beginning a new week. Travelers streamed into town from both the east and west, making their way to and from the port city of Neapolis.

Paul, Silas, Luke and Timothy arrived in the market square around midday, and before long, a crowd had gathered around them. They spoke easily to the residents and travelers. They asked questions and offered their own experiences. Lydia watched from her booth for a while, but as customers came in to shop, she attended to them.

One woman asked if she knew who the men were.

"They are friends of mine. They came to town to bring good news about Jesus of Nazareth." The explanation spilled out of Lydia's mouth without a thought.

"Oh, how interesting," the shopper replied. "Maybe I will go and hear what they have to say."

Lydia smiled and helped her with her purchase, and then watched as she joined the crowd. By late afternoon, Calchas stood in front of his booth with a deep frown engraved on his face.

"What is troubling you, my friend?" Lydia asked.

"These strangers move into our peaceful city and stir up trouble. They take our customers and leave us with empty shops." He gestured to Lydia's booth. "Your place is as empty as ours."

"They bring no trouble, Calchas. They simply share news from my God." She patted his arm and sighed. "Do not worry about Philippi. These men bring only blessings."

"Hmmph, I wonder." His narrow shoulders shrugged above his wide waist. The fabric draped over his left shoulder began to slip, and he quickly pushed it back to its perch.

"Enjoy the quiet moments, friend. I am certain our shops will be busy again very soon." Lydia turned back to her front table as a breeze lifted a piece of cloth and rolled it into a heap. "Even without the crowds, there is always something to keep our hands busy."

When she looked over her shoulder, Calchas had disappeared. She nodded to herself and set her hands to straightening her wares. Marcus had already left for his wrestling match with his friends.

"Listen to these men!" a shrill, high-pitched voice rose from the agora. "They are here to show you the way to the god most high!"

Lydia stood up straight and nearly ran to the front of her booth. She wondered who was yelling. She had never heard the voice before. It sounded like a child or young woman. She scanned the crowd. Suddenly she heard it again.

"These men have news from the most high god! Listen to them!"

Lydia blinked in disbelief. It was Daphne, Calchas' seer, and she was yelling at the top of her lungs. Ercole stood beside her, handing out token rings as he had when Daphne first arrived.

"These men are sent by the highest god!" Her voice was loud and clear above the chatter of the crowds and the speech of Paul and Silas.

"For such a small child, she can certainly make some noise, can she not?" Calchas asked when he saw Lydia staring.

"Yes..." was all that she could manage.

"I am a shrewd businessman. If the crowds do not come

to me, I go to the crowds. She will draw them back here, and I will help them find the way to the god most high." Calchas crossed his arms over his chest and rested them proudly on his belly.

Lydia blinked several times at her associate. "The god most high?" she repeated after Calchas.

"Zeus, of course," he responded. "I have many idols and charms of Zeus. He is the father of the gods. Most powerful indeed."

Bile filled Lydia's throat, and she cringed at the perversion of her friends' message. She shook her head and retreated into her shop. After several more minutes of Daphne's shouting, the crowd dispersed, and Lydia saw Paul and Silas walking north to the theater. Luke and Timothy came to visit her.

"That was quite an experience," Timothy said with a sigh as he greeted Lydia.

"Come in and sit down," she said, gesturing to a small bench against the wall. "I will bring some water."

"Thank you," said Luke. He smiled broadly and took a seat. Turning to Timothy, he said, "My son, you will experience much more than that in our travels."

Lydia brought them water and pushed a straying curl back under her head covering. "Daphne is the fortune teller from the booth next door to mine. Calchas and Ercole sell idols and amulets. They also sell incenses and potions. They call them the spells of Olympus."

Luke nodded. "The Hellenic temple here is much smaller than in some other places where we have been. Philippi has a vast blend of cultures. The fact that it is not unified in one central religion makes our message easier to hear, I think."

Lydia took a deep breath and felt better after seeing him handle the matter with calm composure. "I think everyone in the square could hear the girl."

Timothy nodded and tugged at his ear. "I was standing right next to her when she started yelling. My ears are still ringing."

Luke laughed. "Satan uses many messengers to twist our words. Some are loud and shrill. Some are quiet whispers in the night."

"You are not afraid that they will draw people away from you?" Lydia asked.

"They certainly will. But we are not the message, just the messengers. God will call whom He wishes to call." Luke sipped at his water and handed the cup back to Lydia. "May I see your fabrics?"

"Of course," she said, motioning to the stacks of cloth around the room. "The Tyrian purples are here." She picked up the deepest purple-blue cut of linen. "The dye comes from a mollusk. You can still smell the scent of the sea."

Luke took the roll of cloth from her hands and held it close under his nose. He smiled. "I spent several years in Tarsus learning medicine. This smell reminds me of that time." He carefully put the cloth back into its place. "What about these lighter colors?"

Lydia led him to the pale hues of blues, pinks, and lavenders at the front of the booth. "These are dyed with the oils from the madder flower. The color is not as strong, but neither is the odor." She chuckled.

"And which is your favorite color?" Timothy asked, looking from one item to the next.

Lydia raised her brow and pointed to the roll of soft fabric on the table in the center of the shop. "This one is my favorite. I always keep some here. It is a Tyrian color, but it is dyed in such a way as to create a dark shade of crimson. When I was young—first married—Simeon and I spent hours working together to get this precise color."

"Simeon is your husband?" Timothy asked.

"Yes," she answered. "He died last year. He was quite ill for a few months."

Luke tilted his head and softened his dark brown eyes. "Were many others sick?"

Lydia shook her head. "No, Simeon had gone home to see his mother before she died. He stayed until she was gone, and then a while longer to help his family grieve. By the time he was ready to come back, the weather had turned. He tried to beat the winter storms, but he did not get to sea soon enough. His ship ran aground on the rocks. The cargo was lost, but everyone aboard survived."

She took a few seconds to clear the mist from her eyes. "They all had to walk several miles in the storms to make it to Neapolis. Simeon should have stayed there and rested, but he wanted to come back to me. He walked until he was home, and he collapsed at our door. Three months later he ... died."

Luke and Timothy both had slumped shoulders and downcast faces. "We are sorry," Timothy said with a cough. "I lost my father when I was very young. It is difficult. I know how my mother grieved, too."

Luke raised his chin. "For myself, I take comfort in the words of Jesus. He taught that God's children would have a home with Him in heaven after this life. I hold fast to that hope of again seeing those who have gone before me."

"Thank you." Lydia reached for his hand. "That is a great comfort."

Luke nodded. "Well! Perhaps we should go back to the house and prepare for the gathering. We will pick up some food from the market vendors on our way."

Lydia perked up. "Go to the cart with the dried fish at the end of this row," she said, pointing to the last booth on her left. "Phoebe's uncle owns that one. If you invite him to my home, then he will probably bring his whole family."

Luke held up his hands to the sky as he stepped into the afternoon sun. "Then he is just the man I will see," he said. He placed his hand over her heart. "Thank you, Lydia, for the refreshment and your wisdom. We will see you soon."

Luke and Timothy made their way to the other end of the shops as Lydia began to prepare her booth for closing. Once she had everything put away, she went out to let down the awning.

She noticed a line of visitors in front of Calchas' booth, waiting to go in to see Daphne. Lydia forced a smile and nodded to the chattering customers.

"Such a beautiful girl..."

"So innocent..."

"Blessed by the high priestess..."

"Cannot wait to see what she has to say..."

One after another, they sang the praises of a slave child, forced to take a concoction of herbs to see into the future.

As Lydia prayed silently for a way to reach out to these people, a gust of wind filled the awning and ripped the support pole from her hands, knocking her to the ground.

Two of the young men from the line saw what happened and came to help.

"Are you all right?" one asked, helping her to her feet as the other took control of the post and awning.

"I am. Thank you," she said, trying to catch her breath.

Together the three of them got the awning down and secured. "Can we help you with anything else?" the youth asked again.

Lydia took a deep breath. "No, but I am very grateful for your help. Are you here because of the men who were speaking in the agora today?"

The shorter of the two boys finally spoke. "Yes. We wanted to hear more, but they had to move on. A friend of theirs invited us to come and listen to what the gods say about our future."

Lydia nodded. "Because of me, you lost your place in line, but I can help you. You see, the men who spoke today are staying at my house. They will talk more tonight. I would love to invite you both to join my household for supper and hear what these teachers have to say."

The boys looked at each other with excitement in their eyes. "These same men will be at your house?" the taller one asked.

"Yes, the same men," she said. "My name is Lydia."

The boy looked back to the line and then to his friend. "I am Epaphroditus, and this is Gallus." The taller boy gestured to his friend. He turned back to Lydia. "Where do you live?" he asked.

Lydia grinned. "My home is the one at the south edge of the olive grove. You will know it by the four white columns on the portico."

"The enormous one at the end of the gray stone path?" Epaphroditus asked, in obvious awe. "Then you are a relative of Marcus?"

"Yes, that is my house, and yes, he is my cousin. Will you come?" Lydia smiled, and then added, "You may bring anyone else you like. Everyone is welcome."

"We will be there," Gallus said. "Marcus is a friend of ours." The boys nodded and hurried away.

Lydia squared her shoulders as she started toward home. As she passed the cart owned by Phoebe's uncle, he waved.

"See you tonight, Lydia," he called out.

She waved back and felt a pain in her shoulder. She had not realized before how hard or how quickly the wind had pulled the pole from her grip. She would be sore tomorrow, but she did not care. In a few hours, she would have a busy house.

The thought settled in and filled her heart with delight. She missed having friends and family fill her rooms. She missed celebrations, she missed feeling joy.

But tonight, the joy would return.

SIX

"We brought some more bread, Lydia," Euodia said as her friend, Syntyche, carried a basket through the portico and beyond to the table. "We invited our neighbors, and we wanted to make sure there would be plenty."

Lydia smiled and nodded. "Thank you, dear friend. I believe we have enough now to feed Caesar's own army."

Luke led a small group of guests to the courtyard where Paul and Silas were already speaking. "It *appears* to be plenty," he said with a sly grin, as he passed the women, "but you have never seen Timothy eat."

Lydia laughed. She waited at her entry for another half hour as more people arrived. When she first came home, she feared that her traveling friends might be disappointed with only a few citizens attending. That fear quickly dissipated and another concern replaced it. So many people came to hear their message that she fretted about where to put them all.

Unwilling to be seen as an unprepared host, Lydia immediately invited the guests to her inner courtyard. The open space between her main home, her kitchen, and the stable area stretched out with a lush garden edging. Simeon had spent a month building benches around the area a few years ago. Though he was gone, Lydia felt his presence everywhere she looked.

Once everyone was inside, Lydia joined the group. She found a seat near the back of the crowd, where she could welcome any latecomers if necessary.

Paul was already talking about his encounter with Jesus. He told about being struck blind in the middle of the road. The crowd gasped.

Lydia listened to the story again, but this time she felt an urge to pray. This was not a prayer of joy or thanksgiving—though she felt both. Her heart suddenly weighed heavy in her chest. Her eyes burned with unbidden tears. *What is this?*

She stood, almost without thinking, and hurried back to her portico. She went to the nearest column and held fast to the cold marble. She did not understand what was happening, but she had to pray.

"O God, mighty Creator of the earth and everything in it, hear my heart as I cry out," she whispered through sobs. "O Lord, have mercy on me as I search for words—as I search for direction. I feel Your calling, and I long to hear Your voice. You fulfill the desires of the righteous. Lord, help me to be righteous in Your eyes. My hope is in You. Open my heart and my eyes to know what You would have me do."

She continued for several minutes more, moving her lips in a silent request. The longer she prayed, the easier the tears flowed. She still had no idea why she felt overcome, but as the troubles of her heart overflowed, Lydia felt as if she was doing something important.

As the last of the sunlight began to sink beyond the horizon, Lydia looked up to Mount Orbelos. The peak shone a glistening pink, and a halo of gold-tinted clouds crept around the mountain's shoulders. She watched the sky turn from a silvery blue to a pale purple. Silent awe filled her thoughts. She heard nothing but the soft wind in the grove and a bird singing from far away.

From within her home, she heard a man's voice begin to sing. She recognized that it was Silas. His strong melody carried through the evening air, and soon others in the crowd joined him.

Lydia felt her shoulders begin to relax. The music filled her whole house as it had years before when Simeon would sing. She felt comfortable and smiled as she listened.

"He is blessed with a pleasant tone," Luke said from behind her.

Lydia spun to face him, and a blush rose in her cheeks. "I was praying," she started to explain.

"I saw you," he replied. He gestured softly with his hands. "I saw you leave the courtyard. You appeared upset, and I wanted to make sure that you were well."

Lydia nodded. "I am. I do not know why, but I had to come away and pray." She wiped at the dried tear streaks on her cheeks. "Nothing like that has ever happened to me before."

"I think when you feel the Spirit prompting, you should obey," he said. His dark eyes calmed and reassured her.

"That was the Spirit?" she asked.

Luke nodded and gestured to the bench against the outside wall. He took her elbow and helped her sit before taking his place beside her. "The Spirit prompts and guides us in many ways. Some ways are easy to identify. Others may be more difficult. But I find that if I ever have an over-whelming urge to pray, the Spirit is certainly behind it."

"It has happened to you?" she asked, curious about his experience.

"Quite often, in fact."

"What happens? I mean, what happens when *you* pray?"

Luke's eyes sparked a smile that spread over his whole face. From within the house, they could hear the song rise and fall, as more and more voices learned the song and joined in.

Luke looked up to the high ceiling of the portico and sighed. "All I can tell you is that something happens. I do not always get to know about it at the time, but *something always happens* when I pray."

Lydia knit her brows together. "What does that mean?"

Luke shrugged. "Sometimes when I pray, I see God's answers right away. Sometimes the answers are as plain as the sky." He gestured to the purple-blue canopy that dark-ened above them. "Other times I pray, and the answers seem to come slowly, or not at all. But I have faith that God has a plan that grows." He leaned back and crossed his arms over his chest. "When I was a youth, I wanted nothing more than to be a grown man, but the days passed slowly."

"And now?" she asked.

"Now I can see how quickly the years raced away. It is that way with prayer, sometimes. I cannot always see an answer until I look back."

"And what if I do not know what to pray?" Lydia asked, almost embarrassed that she still did not understand.

Luke faced her and fixed his eyes on hers. His expression became serious.

Lydia's heart pounded in her throat, and she felt as though she might burst into tears again.

"That is when the Spirit is most present." Luke's voice rose barely above a whisper. "The prayers you say, when you have no words, are most precious. The Spirit takes them to the Lord and pours out every feeling at His feet. Your prayer becomes a lovely aroma in God's nose."

Lydia clasped her hands tightly together and swallowed hard. "What will happen?"

Luke took a breath and straightened his shoulders. "We will see. God is moving in Philippi in a powerful way. I did not expect this crowd already, did you?"

Lydia shook her head. "No."

Luke smiled and stood. The song faded, and Paul began speaking again. "One thing we can be sure about," Luke said, "is that God will not always do *what* we expect, but He will always do *more* than we expect."

Lydia rose to her feet and smiled. "I am anxious to see what He will do here."

Luke grimaced. "Do not be anxious. Be open. You will see amazing things. You will see tragic things. If you watch carefully, then you will see miracles, as I have."

Lydia wanted to ask more, but she could see that her guests were up and moving about the courtyard. Luke pointed inside. "We will be needed very soon."

As they started in, Lydia caught Mary running past the door.

"Mary, what is it?" Lydia asked.

"A dozen people are going to be baptized. I am going to fetch the towels." She spoke too quickly and ran out of air before she was finished.

"Go on, then," Lydia said, patting her shoulder. "Slow down, though. You do not want to hurt anyone—least of all yourself."

Luke laughed. "She is excited. I am as well."

"What shall we do?" Lydia asked. "Should I invite people to stay to eat?"

Luke held out his hands. "Food always provides an opportunity for fellowship, but you know these people better than anyone else. What do they need?"

Lydia thought about her guests for a moment, contemplating how best to serve them. She took a deep breath and placed her hand on Luke's wrist, leading him to where Phoebe's uncle was standing. "Alexander, I am very pleased that you came and brought your dear wife with you. Have you met my friend, Luke? He is a physician, traveling with Paul."

Phoebe's uncle, Alexander, eyed Luke and nodded. "A doctor, you say? I met him this afternoon at my booth. A fine man—honest. I should have guessed he was a doctor."

Luke nodded in respect. "I thank you for your kind words."

Alexander raised an eyebrow and twisted his lips as if he was solving a puzzle in his head. Finally, he threw his shoulders back and raised his chin high. He turned to his wife. "He is a learned man, Theda. They all are educated. Paul saw this man, Jesus, with his own eyes."

Luke nodded. "Yes, Silas and I both saw him as well."

"Their testimony has convinced me. What do you think?" Alexander asked. He stared at Theda intently.

She merely sighed. "I think we should find Paul. Phoebe was right. I heard their story, and I want to be baptized, too."

Lydia took Theda's hand and led the couple to the stable where Paul was already at the trough with others.

As Theda and Alexander waited, Luke turned back to Lydia. "I will wait here until Silas and Timothy come out. You should return to the house and see if anyone else wants to be baptized tonight."

Lydia's heart felt warm as she returned to the courtyard and sought out others. Several were already at the table preparing to eat, and she let Agatha and Joel attend to them.

She took Phoebe aside and whispered in her ear. "Your aunt and uncle are at the stables with Paul being baptized. You have been invited to join them. Will you consider it?"

Phoebe's expression exploded with joy. She kissed Lydia on the cheek and disappeared through the archway.

Lydia encouraged her friends to enjoy the food and then went back to the courtyard. She found a young woman sitting alone on a bench on the far side of the garden, hiding her face in her hands. As Lydia approached, she quickly straightened up and dabbed at her face with the back of her wrists. Lydia smiled softly, guessing the girl was no more than seventeen or eighteen years old.

"What is it?" Lydia asked, taking a seat beside her. "May I help?"

The girl shrugged. Lydia could see that she had not regained her composure yet.

"I am Lydia. This is my home. I would like to help if I can."

"My name is Korinna." A shudder raced down her back, and she laughed through a nervous cough. "Pardon my rudeness."

Lydia blinked. "Tears do not arise from lack of manners, dear one. You need not apologize."

"Thank you for your kindness," Korinna said. "I am not sure why I came. I heard the men speaking in the forum this afternoon. I wondered if there was more. I came, and now I cannot leave." She laughed again, holding up her palms as if in surrender.

Lydia looked deep into her black eyes and saw unfathomable fear. She knew that kind of fear. At once, she felt as if this was the very soul for whom she had prayed on the portico.

Without hesitation, Lydia began to speak. She barely had to think about what to say; the words were already spilling out. "I have been afraid for a very long time. When my husband died, I was afraid of being alone. I was afraid because everything was different. I did not know if I could manage without him. He was my foundation, and suddenly I found myself on shifting sand."

Korinna had a look of bewilderment on her face. Her jaw

dropped and tears flooded over her cheeks. "How did you know that my husband was... dead?"

Lydia wrapped her arms around Korinna's shoulders and began to cry with her. After their tears dried, they sat for several more minutes in silence. Lydia felt another tugging on her heart.

She took Korinna's hand in hers. "O Lord, who knows our needs before we ask, You know the desires of our hearts before we recognize them ourselves. Lord, you have brought me a friend in Korinna. I thank You for her. I bless Your name. You saw my needs, and you answered my prayers. Lord, I ask that You make me a servant to Korinna, that I may bless her as You have blessed me."

As Lydia finished the prayer, Korinna shook her head. "I have never had faith in any god. My husband and my parents hoped in Zeus, but I never saw Zeus do anything for anybody."

Lydia listened as she continued. "Tonight, I heard their stories, and I wondered. I wondered, but I still doubted. How could there be a God—a true God that cared for me enough to become flesh and die? I prayed to this invisible God. I asked for something."

"What did you ask of Him?"

Korinna shook her head. "This will sound like foolishness, but I do not know."

Lydia smiled and swallowed a lump rising in her throat. "And earlier I prayed a prayer for someone I did not know."

"I think God answered my prayer," Korinna whispered, squeezing Lydia's hand.

"Mine, too." Lydia smiled and rose to her feet. "Would you like something to eat?"

Korinna nodded and stood beside her new friend. As soon as she did, Lydia saw that Korinna was expecting a baby.

Lydia gasped in surprise, clasping her hands over her heart. "A baby? My precious friend," she exclaimed.

Korinna placed her hand at her side. "In just three months, I will be a mother. I wish my mother were still here with me."

Lydia led her to the table and helped her sit down. "I know that I am not your mother, but I would like to fill that role for you until your baby comes and to provide whatever you may need."

Lydia caught Luke's arm as he finally joined the ongoing meal. She gestured to Korinna. "Luke, this is my new friend, Korinna. After we eat, I would like for you to talk with us for a while."

Luke nodded to the young woman. "I would be happy to speak with you." He took a seat near Timothy and began to eat.

Lydia whispered to Korinna. "Luke is a doctor." She made sure that Korinna got plenty to eat. She spent the meal asking questions about the girl's family and her past.

Korinna seemed more comfortable as the crowd grew smaller. Lydia could ask more about details of her life and found that Korinna had taken a job at an inn after her husband died. The innkeeper gave her room and board in exchange for her cleaning services.

"And how much longer do you think you can keep

cleaning at the inn?" Lydia asked. "That is difficult work for an expectant mother."

Korinna shrugged. "I cannot think about that. I will work as long as I possibly can."

"Can you sew?" Agatha asked the girl, catching a bit of the conversation.

Korinna nodded. "My mother taught me to sew when I was just a small child."

Agatha nudged Lydia. "You should ask if she could help me with the pieces for your shop. I am always behind, and as soon as I have anything made, it sells right away. With another hand helping, we could do much more."

Lydia tilted her head toward the girl. "Sewing is much easier work than cleaning. Would you consider it?"

Korinna started to answer but hesitated. "The inn keepers are kind. They gave me a room..."

Agatha patted Korinna's shoulder. "There is an empty room next to mine, dear. We can get you settled into it tomorrow if you like."

Korinna reached out for Agatha's hand. "Tomorrow? I would love to live here, but I would not want to be a burden."

Lydia shook her head. "You would be a blessing to my home, not a burden at all."

The young woman nodded. "Then yes, I would love to come and work here with you."

Lydia smiled. "Are we all decided?" she asked.

Korinna nodded, and Agatha winked at Lydia.

Lydia gestured to Joel. "I will have Joel and his son send word to the innkeeper right away. They can retrieve your things as well."

"I have never stayed in a house with so much space," Korinna said.

Lydia sighed and stared at the lamp stand on the opposite side of the room. "When Simeon and I built this house, we intended to fill it with children." She let her gaze wander back to her guests around the table. She noticed Luke listening to her intently. "We make plans, but things never seem to unfold as we expect."

Lydia's eyes settled on Korinna. *A baby.* As she stared at her new friend, Lydia's heart fluttered with a mixture of joy and heartache. All the things she had wished for herself, she now wished for Korinna. All the things she had faced by herself as a young widow without family nearby, she now feared for Korinna.

CHAPTER

SEVEN

The next two days followed roughly the same pattern. Lydia went to her shop for the day, and the four travelers went to the forum to speak. After a crowd had gathered to hear their message, Calchas sent Daphne into the throng to begin her barking. Once she reached the point that the whole crowd could hear her advertising Calchas' shop and wares, Paul and his companions moved on to the theater to continue their preaching.

Marcus's attitude remained cool and business-like with Lydia. He kept his conversation with her to a minimum and joined his friends each afternoon for a wrestling match or two.

At dusk Lydia's house filled with friends and neighbors, all of whom wanted to hear more of Paul's witness. Epaphroditus and Gallus, the two youths who had helped Lydia with her awning, came each night and were soon baptized. Paul baptized Korinna on the second night of meeting. Marcus stayed in his room in the evenings, doing his best to avoid the gatherings entirely. Lydia invited him to join the group, even if only for a meal, but Marcus refused.

The third morning began in the same way, but Lydia sensed that something was different before she even left her home. As the guests ate their small morning meals, she could see a look of expectation in their eyes. Though their conversation sounded unremarkable, the way they spoke caused Lydia to think they might be planning something different for today's message.

The shoppers began arriving at Lydia's booth early. Several asked if Paul was going to speak again. Lydia assured them that he would be there.

When the men arrived, Paul strode straight up to the center of the raised platform in front of the magistrate's building, where all of Philippi's public announcements were made. Though it was not elevated more than a foot or two above ground level, the dais had been constructed precisely to allow the speaker's voice to carry over crowds.

And it was a crowd that formed as soon as Paul began to speak. Lydia went to the front of her booth to watch. To her surprise, she could hear Paul's voice clearly from across the whole agora. She saw Silas and Timothy move through the people, answering questions and inviting them to the evening meeting. She stood up on her toes and scanned the crowd for Luke but could not find him.

"Are you looking for me?" his voice drifted from behind her, giving her a start.

She could hear the smile in his words before she turned to face him. "Yes, I was."

"I thought today I would watch from your booth."

Lydia raised her eyebrow, wondering what to expect, as Paul continued his message to the city.

"The builders of your fair city," Paul said, his words sounding clear from dozens of yards away. "They used their education and skills to construct a mighty theater." He gestured to the north. "They built a palaestra for sports." He motioned to the fields at his right. "They made this forum to be a great meeting place, where people can come together and exchange their goods, their ideas, and their stories. But truly, one of the jewels in the crown of this city is the public latrines just off the highway behind me." He turned his head to gesture to the road at his left.

The people in the crowd nodded and laughed. All travelers who frequented the Via Egnatia knew that Philippi boasted of her luxurious public baths and modern latrines.

Paul continued. "Your engineers and craftsmen all acknowledged the nature of man. They sought a way to remove the stench and filth of the human condition. They used the most contemporary methods of sanitation to provide citizens and strangers alike the means to cleanse their bodies of the waste that is common to us all."

The people chattered to each other, wondering where this line of thought might carry him.

Paul raised his hands to the sky. "The one, true, and holy God of creation knows the condition of our souls. He alone has the means to cleanse us of our filth and waste. I do not mean the physical excrement, but the spiritual waste and desolation that our willful hearts create."

An excited hum rose from the listeners as they begin to understand.

"We yearn to be clean, and God provides us with a way," Paul added.

Lydia chuckled. "That certainly got their attention."

Luke laughed. "He is a shrewd speaker. He knows what will stir his audience to respond."

Just then, the now-familiar screech of Daphne's voice began. "Listen to these men!" she cried out. "They have a message for you from the highest god!"

Luke released a low, tense breath. "It is time."

Lydia faced him and tilted her head as she saw the intense stare in his eyes. "Time for what?"

Luke took a step toward the crowd and waited. "Paul is not going to allow her to continue this anymore."

Lydia saw Silas move behind Daphne and Ercole as they stood in the center of the crowd, waving their hands to attract attention. Daphne carried on with her yelling.

"What will he do?" Lydia asked. She knew that Paul would not hurt her, but she wondered how anyone would go about quieting such a clamor.

Luke started to speak, but before he could say a word, Paul was reaching toward Daphne and speaking in a thunderous tone. "I call out to the demons that hold this child in their grasp," he yelled. "In the name of Jesus, the Christ, I command you to release her!"

The mass became silent. Daphne stopped, mid-scream, and dropped to her knees, shaking. In another second, she was lying still on her back, as if asleep. Ercole growled at the people around them, demanding that they step back from the girl.

Silas knelt at her side and began to pray, but Ercole pushed him away.

Lydia clutched her hands together over her heart, speechless at what she saw. Luke nodded to himself, searching the forum for Timothy.

Lydia saw Calchas bounce from his seat at the door of his booth into the commotion of the mob. "What has he done? What has he done?" she heard him say.

Luke placed his hand gently on Lydia's shoulder. "She will be all right now," he assured her. "For her whole life, this girl has been fed laurel leaves to keep her a captive."

Lydia knit her brows. "But laurel is poisonous."

"Yes, when enough is ingested, it kills," Luke explained. "But when small amounts are eaten over time, the body builds a resistance to it. The poison becomes a way to control. It causes visions—terrible visions. The girl has been a slave and prisoner to the demons that her owners feed and keep alive in her mind."

Lydia shrugged. "I do not understand."

Luke nodded. "Through Paul, God has released her from the poisonous demon. She will no longer be a slave to the terror. She will be all right."

Calchas screamed as he picked up his prized possession and carried the girl back to his booth. Ercole hissed and roared at everyone around him. He began to swear by the gods of Olympus, calling down curses upon Paul and Silas.

Luke gestured to Lydia as Calchas stomped past them. "He may listen to you."

"What?" she asked. She wanted to help Daphne, but what could she do? Calchas and Ercole were her friends—her associates. She did not want to step between them and Paul and Silas. What could she say to Calchas that would calm his rage?

She stared at Luke, and he seemed to be waiting patiently for her to come around and agree. She did not want to confront Calchas, but somehow Luke's suggestion made sense. Who else could help the girl? Who else would?

Lydia's eyes widened, and she drew a deep breath. She took a step toward the front of her neighbor's booth. "Calchas, may I help you? Can I bring some water for Daphne?"

As she took another step into his booth, she saw Calchas pushing a handful of crushed laurel leaves into Daphne's mouth.

"Chew, girl. Take them; eat," he demanded.

The rag doll of a child tried to swallow, but could not manage it. Instead, a stream of vomit poured from her lips and covered her master.

Calchas jumped to his feet, enraged. Ercole picked up a nearby cup and forced it to Daphne's mouth. The pale green liquid from the vessel spilled down the front of her tunic, and she began to retch.

"If she cannot take the potions, she cannot see the future!" Ercole whined.

"I know," Calchas bellowed. He threw off his soiled himation and scraped at his tunic. "Those wretched men have made her less than worthless to me."

Lydia raised her hand. "May I tend to her?" she asked

again. She reached out to Daphne, but Calchas batted at her gesture.

"Get away from us, Lydia!" Ercole said. "It is your friends who have ruined our property."

Lydia dropped her hands to her side, but she kept eye contact with Daphne, hoping to calm her. "She is afraid, Calchas. Please let me help her."

"She should be afraid," Calchas said, to both Lydia and Daphne. "She should fear for her life." He was more than angry. Wrath saturated his words and his expression. His face flushed red, and the veins at his temples swelled and throbbed so that Lydia could see them. "If she cannot see the future for our customers, her days are at an end," he growled.

Daphne's expression turned to terror. Her eyes pleaded silently with Lydia for help.

Calchas paced as Ercole stomped around the shop like a child in the middle of a tantrum. Lydia could no longer wait for permission. She raced to Daphne's side and wrapped her arm around the girl's shoulder for comfort.

"You will be all right soon," she whispered. She could feel Daphne's frail body trembling in her arms. "Everything will be fine."

Calchas pointed to Ercole. "You stay here and close up the shop. I am going to see Takis."

Lydia watched as the round man stomped away into the center of the crowd that still surrounded Paul. He caught hold of Silas's arm and dragged him along to the far side of the forum.

"Takis!" Calchas called out. A tall, angular man stepped into the sunlight from the shadows of his doorway. Takis was the magistrate of Philippi, and he walked slowly and precisely, reminding everyone who saw him that he was in charge.

"Calchas, brother, what is wrong?" Takis asked in a deep, pronounced voice.

"These men have taken my seer's ability from her. My business is ruined because of them." Calchas pushed Silas forward and to the ground into Takis' view. Paul boldly stepped forward and helped his friend back to his feet.

Takis eyed the two strangers with skepticism. "You are not from Philippi?" he questioned them.

Calchas shook his head and interrupted. "I am a leading citizen of this city!" he shouted. "I accuse them of stirring up trouble. Of denouncing the gods of Rome, herself. Of defiling my property and making it useless to me!" He turned to Paul and Silas and placed his hands where his hips might have been. "Do you deny this?"

Paul took a deep breath and faced Takis. "We do not deny any of his accusations," he began. Calchas cut off any explanation Paul or Silas might offer.

"I demand that they are flogged immediately!" Calchas growled.

Takis snapped his fingers toward a small company of soldiers. They leaped into action. Four of them used their spears to push back the crowds, while another four took Paul and Silas forcibly and began stripping their robes and tunics from their bodies. When the travelers' backs were bared, another two soldiers stepped forward with whips and started beating them without hearing their defense.

Ercole began closing their booth, and Lydia scooped

Daphne into her arms and pulled her to the doorway in the front where the child could feel the warmth of the sun upon her face.

"Calchas will bring the whole city of Philippi down on your friends," Ercole spat at Lydia. "He spent a full year's profit on the girl, and he will never forgive this treachery."

Lydia raked Daphne's hair back from her face and held the girl's shoulders. "And what treacheries have they committed?" she asked. Lydia could see the soldiers' whips flying above the heads of the onlookers. She could hear Paul and Silas groaning after each strike. She winced in sympathy and turned her attention toward Daphne. Color began to fill the girl's cheeks, and her eyes seemed to turn a vibrant, focused green.

Ercole tramped to her side and waggled his finger in her face. "He stole the power of visions from this child. Just look at her. *Look at her!* She's broken. Useless."

Lydia looked again into Daphne's eyes. She still saw fear, but the foggy cloud that had enveloped Daphne just a few minutes ago was gone.

Lydia turned back to face Luke, who stood silently at the door of her booth. He fixed his eyes on Paul and Silas as they endured the public beating. Lydia saw his lips moving and knew he was praying.

She looked directly into Ercole's face. "Can a mere man steal power like that?" she asked plainly. Her heart pounded so loudly that she could barely hear the commotion in the forum. She startled herself with the boldness in her voice.

Ercole shook his head. "I have not seen that before. Perhaps he called on one of his gods," he suggested.

"He has but one God, Ercole. He worships only the Creator of the Universe." She helped Daphne to sit upright and encouraged her to take deep breaths.

"I bow to Zeus as well," he replied.

"Not Zeus, Ercole. He worships Jehovah God. The Hebrew God."

Ercole spat on the ground as he lowered the awning of his shop. "And now look at her," he repeated. "Worthless."

Lydia felt Daphne's hands grip at her *peplos*, or dress. Lydia patted her shoulder and nodded to calm her. Lydia rose slightly, just to her knees, and stared shamelessly at Ercole. She tried to suppress the thought forming in her mind, but the stronger she fought, the more fiercely the words pushed out from her lips. "Why not call on *your* gods to give her back the vision?"

Daphne pulled away from her and trembled. She shook her head at Lydia and tears began to flood over her cheeks.

Luke turned to face Lydia with his brows raised high at her suggestion.

Ercole waved his arms in frustration. "I am certain that Calchas will do exactly that when he is finished with your friends." Ercole shot a severe glance at Luke. "You should be glad that you were here when all of this happened, or you would be suffering the same fate as they are."

Luke reached down to help both Lydia and Daphne to their feet, but Ercole pushed him away with one swift hand to the center of Luke's chest. Without a word, Luke raised his hands and stepped back.

Lydia adjusted the folds of her peplos so she could stand; and, once upright, she helped Daphne to her feet. She squeezed the girl's hand for reassurance. "I will not allow them to hurt you."

With both hands, Daphne squeezed Lydia's wrist. "I am afraid," the girl said in a raspy whisper.

Ercole glared at the crowd and then back at Lydia. "You cannot stop Calchas from rebuilding his business," he hissed. He narrowed his eyes and leaned toward Daphne. "By whatever means necessary. You will return to your trance, girl."

Another wave of tears poured over her cheeks, and the child buried her face into Lydia's shoulder.

Lydia scowled at Ercole but turned to face the forum when the crowd seemed to swell in a collective moan. "What is happening?" she asked Luke.

"Silas is losing consciousness. His lashing is finished. Both soldiers are on Paul now, but he only has a few blows left." Luke inhaled a deep breath. "It is over now."

"Far from over," Ercole growled. "They will be jailed and put on trial right away. Calchas will have his revenge. This kind of insult may demand crucifixion."

Lydia took advantage of the distraction and inched Daphne and herself away from Ercole. The closer they got to Lydia's booth, the more color returned to Daphne's face.

Luke lifted his chin to reassure Lydia. "Stay with the child for as long as you can," he instructed. "Timothy and I will see to the others. Go back home when Calchas orders you to do so." He tilted his chin to Daphne. "Do not be afraid. The God who saved you will deliver you still."

Lydia nodded and watched him disappear into the mob. She held Daphne close and kept her tone soft. "I will stay as long as I can. You must do whatever Calchas asks of you without resisting. His poisons will not take hold of you again."

Daphne shuddered within Lydia's grasp. "He will kill me."

Lydia shook her head. "No. You cannot think like that. He will need to keep you alive to speak at trial."

"Why did they do this for me? If they have the power to take away my visions, why did they not use that power to save themselves from the beating?" Daphne asked. She watched Ercole pacing like a hungry tiger. She tightened her grasp of Lydia's arm.

Lydia put her free hand to Daphne's cheek. "They do not order God around like a slave. They ask in faith and receive what God is pleased to give. You, child, are favored to receive."

Ercole scoffed. "You are nothing to be favored. You are not a citizen; you are property to be used. Calchas is your god." He waved his arms toward the crowd. "Here comes your god now."

CHAPTER

EIGHT

Lydia and Agatha waited at the door as a few believers arrived for nightly prayers. Each person asked about the well-being of Paul and Silas and whether Takis would release the men from jail soon.

"I have heard nothing yet," Lydia explained. "Calchas demanded that they be confined, and Takis obliged without question. Calchas and Ercole took the girl Daphne home. They believe they can restore her visions."

"What can we do?" Alexander asked when he heard the news.

Lydia shook her head. "We can pray. We must wait for instruction." She looked around for Alexander's family. "Where is Theda? Phoebe wants to talk to her."

Alexander dropped his head. "I told her to stay home tonight. This kind of thing raises fears for my household."

"I understand," Lydia answered. "Come inside and speak with Phoebe. She will be glad to see your face."

Agatha appraised the smaller crowd. "I think perhaps many are afraid to meet tonight after what happened this afternoon."

Luke and Timothy appeared on the path and joined them. Timothy took Agatha's hand and led her inside. "We need to gather a few things to take to the jail for Paul and Silas," he explained as they left Lydia and Luke at the door.

Luke fixed a sturdy smile to his lips as he faced Lydia, staring into her dark brown eyes. "How are you?" he finally asked.

Lydia realized that she had been holding her breath, and she released a heavy sigh. Her vision blurred for a moment, and she reached out for Luke's hand. Until that moment, she had not given herself a second thought.

"You are trembling." Luke reached out to steady her. "Have you eaten?"

"No, I could not manage anything. I can only think of what happened to Paul and Silas and what may be happening to Daphne as we speak." She suddenly felt the warmth of Luke's grasp as he circled his arm around her and led her to the bench.

"We will go inside, and while I talk to the gathering, you find something to eat. I want you to take some food to the jail tonight. The magistrate—Takis, is it? —agreed to allow us to bring them supper." As he spoke to Lydia his expression lightened, and a sincere smile formed on his face.

She noticed and glanced down at his hands covering hers. She missed a man's touch and felt safe with Luke. She raised her eyes. "Will you go with me to the jail?"

"We shall see," Luke replied. He stood again and gestured

toward the kitchen. Lydia nodded and left his side, feeling steadier on her feet.

Once in the kitchen, Lydia found Phoebe chopping cucumbers and crying. "What is it?" Lydia asked, placing her hand on her maidservant's shoulder.

Phoebe set her knife down and shrugged. "Alexander and Theda are scared. Even Joel is afraid for the children and me. They think this message may bring death to us all." She hugged Lydia. "What can I say to calm them?"

Lydia shook her head. "If you saw what I saw this afternoon," she began, but then paused. She struggled to form the right words. "Paul called the demons out of the child, and she was healed. In the blink of an eye, she was healed." She swallowed against her swelling emotions. "He cast out the demons in the name of Jesus. Phoebe, he was not afraid of what would happen to him. He practically asked to be flogged."

"It must have been awful," Phoebe sobbed.

Lydia tilted her head, deep in thought. *It should have been awful, but somehow it was wonderful.* She released a short sigh. "And Luke watched from my side, all the time praying. As Silas suffered, Luke remained strong. Timothy stood ready for whatever the others needed."

"You must have been scared to death."

Lydia shook her head. "I was—that is, I might have been frightened, but Daphne needed someone to care for her. I was at her side, and somehow my fears did not matter."

Phoebe widened her eyes. "You are a strong woman."

Lydia shook her head as she ate a few slices of cucumber and a small portion of bread. "I think that following Jesus will require all of us to become strong. But if today is an example of how God works through us, I can say that He will provide all of the strength we will need."

"He will," Luke said as he strode into the room. "It is growing late. Have you prepared something for our friends?"

Lydia searched the small kitchen, examining the things Timothy and Agatha included in the basket. "Do you think this will be enough?" she asked.

Luke quickly examined the contents of the woven bin. "Fish, bread, cheese, fruit—yes it will be sufficient." He looked Lydia over. "Do you have any jewelry that you could use to bribe the jailer if necessary?"

Phoebe raised her eyebrows and took a step backward toward the door. "What?" she asked.

Lydia barely blinked. "I have two gold bangles on my dressing table." She waved at her servant. "Phoebe, please run up and get them."

Phoebe nodded in a fog of bewilderment. "Yes, Mistress," she said and then quickly disappeared from the room.

"Do you expect I will need more than that?" she asked.

Luke shook his head. "No, if you take too much, someone will start to believe their prisoners are important. It would never do to have them asking after our friends in the wrong circles."

"I hate seeing people like Paul and Silas being beaten like that." Lydia covered the food and wrapped the basket for easy carrying. "Philippi is usually a peaceful place, and we save flogging for people who actually do something evil."

Luke almost chuckled. "Paul should be used to flogging

by now." He turned to the window next to the worktable. "Your magistrate's soldiers did no worse than others."

Lydia's face contorted as she imagined worse than the flogging she witnessed earlier. "Others?"

"Paul has been stoned and left for dead on more than one occasion already. I cannot count how many times he has been under the whip."

"How dreadful," she whispered. Lydia pulled her shawl up over her hair and secured it with her pin. "This is a common treatment for followers of Jesus?"

"Well," Luke began, looking pensively toward the ceiling, "it is common treatment for Paul."

When Phoebe returned, she thrust the bracelets into Lydia's hands with a quick, "Here, Mistress."

"Thank you, Phoebe." She pushed the bangles onto her arms and picked up the basket of supper. "I am just about ready to go." She motioned toward the portico, and Luke followed her out the front door.

The sky was dark, and the insects chirped their evening songs. Lydia looked up into Luke's tender eyes. "You are not going with me, are you?"

"No. After speaking with some of the men, I am concerned that Takis and perhaps a few others expect Timothy or me to try to free our friends from their cells. If you go alone, they will not suspect such things. I do not believe anyone will treat you harshly." He gently pushed back a stray curl from in front of her eyes. "You will be safe."

Lydia smiled and nodded. "Will you lead the group in prayer for me, and for Paul and Silas?" she asked him.

"Of course, I will," he said with a tender smile. "May I pray for you now, before you leave?"

"Yes, please." She swallowed a lump in her throat.

Luke led her a few steps to the bench and motioned for her to sit. He placed one hand on her shoulder and raised his other hand to the sky. "Lord God, King of all creation, hear your humble servant as he asks for mercies. Bless your servants, Paul and Silas as they suffer for Your glory. Preserve them, if it is Your will, that they may continue to tell others of Your mighty works and Your boundless grace." Luke paused and held fast to Lydia. He lowered his hand to touch the crown of her head.

"Lord Jehovah," he continued, "You have blessed your servants with this woman who has offered herself to You and her home to Your work. She has held back nothing from You, Lord. Your servant asks that You protect Lydia tonight as she takes food to Paul and Silas. Lord, use her to further Your kingdom and guide her steps as You reveal the path You place before her."

Lydia nodded in agreement with the prayer.

"In the precious name of Jesus," he said, waiting for her voice to join his.

"Amen."

Luke helped her to her feet. "Do you want to take Agatha or Phoebe with you?" he asked.

"No, I do not want the others to think I am afraid. I would rather have them here with you, praying." Lydia reached up to the shelf at the side of the door where her lantern was perched. "I will take my lamp and go alone." She held the basket of food with one arm and the lantern with the other.

Luke nodded. "It is okay to feel afraid, you know?"

"I know, Luke," she said, taking the first step off her porch. "But the Lord is my shepherd."

Luke smiled at her courage. "We will pray and wait for your return."

NINE

The oil lantern swayed back and forth as Lydia walked the narrow road to Philippi's center. The trees on either side of her reached their thick black branches into the purple sky. She recalled her childhood, and how her mother told her that the highest tips of the tallest trees would poke their sharp ends through the canopy, allowing the light of the heavens to shine through to brighten the earth. She grinned at a simpler time. She could hear the soft hoots of night owls and the crackling twigs snapping under the weight of other creatures in the darkness. She knew what animals lived nearby, and she knew that if she kept to the road, she would be safe from their advances.

In a quarter of an hour, she reached the edge of the forum square. The shops were all asleep, and the only other movement she could see was of a pair of stray dogs making their nightly rounds. At the sight of her lantern, they quickly disappeared.

Lydia walked north through the forum to the wide, paved road. In the distance, she could see lights moving through the columns of the Hellenic temple like fireflies through the trees in late summer. She wondered if Marcus was there now.

"It must be nearly midnight," she whispered, and the sound of her own voice startled her in the silence. For some reason, she could no longer hear any noises from the trees around her. Even the crickets had stopped chirping.

The prison was on the other side of the road. As Lydia descended the marble steps leading from the main highway to the large building's entrance, she thought she could hear singing.

"Yes, that is certainly Silas I hear," she said aloud. His voice chanted out a song of praise.

"To the most high God, creator of the earth," he sang out.

She smiled as she took her last step down the stairway and raised the lamp to the peg at the door. Before she could hang the lantern and knock, she felt her feet shift against her will. She knew instantly what was happening and took several steps away from the building.

Earthquakes were not uncommon in Philippi, but Lydia had never experienced one in the middle of the night while walking alone.

The earth turned to liquid beneath her feet, the dirt shifting and separating from its rocky foundation. She reached out and stumbled, desperate for solid footing. Her lantern flickered and went out as a cloud of dust seemed to rise all around and snuff its light. The chairs and a small table that stood against the courtyard wall rattled and fell over. A tall cypress tree swayed behind her. She turned to see if it was coming down, but without the lamp all she could see was darkness.

The quake seemed to last several minutes. Lydia could hear shouts emanating from inside the prison. As her eyes began to adjust, she saw the forged doors of the jailhouse swing open. The squeal and screech of twisting metal from the iron bars on the cells told Lydia that all the prisoners would soon be freed. With nothing solid to help her balance, Lydia struggled to remain upright. The smell of churning dirt settled hard in her nose, and the rise and fall of the earth made her dizzy and nauseated. She retched.

The quake subsided, and the ground returned to a familiar, stable state. Lydia calmed herself, wiped her mouth, breathed a heavy sigh and picked up the basket of food that she had lost in the chaos. She managed to find her darkened lantern and retreated to a concealed corner, watching the doorway to see who might come out.

Only the jailer, a giant of a man called Arsene, came to the door. He was muttering curses under his breath. Lydia heard him cry out, "By the hand of Zeus, Takis will take my head. The prisoners have all fled."

Lydia could see Arsene drawing his sword from its sheath as he paced. He looked around him, searching for something. The man appeared confused and distraught. He held out his sword as if he intended to fall upon it.

She started to call out to him, but another voice from within the jail stopped him.

"We are all here!" She heard Paul's hoarse voice. "Not one has escaped! Do not hurt yourself!"

Arsene froze in place.

Lydia took a step toward him, holding out her hands, prepared to do whatever she must.

"Who is there?" Arsene asked, turning back into the jail cells. Within a few minutes, Lydia saw the jailer walk past the door again, this time carrying a torch instead of his sword.

Lydia dropped to her knees to pray as she heard several men's voices within the cells. "Thank you, God in heaven, for protecting the men."

"Who is out here?" she heard Arsene call out. He held the torch out to the small courtyard so he could see her.

"I am Lydia," she said as loud as her trembling voice allowed. "I came to bring a small meal to some of the prisoners." She marveled at her own confidence. A week ago, she could never have imagined doing any of this.

"Where is your lamp?" Arsene asked.

"It went out when the earth shook." She took another step toward the door and held the lantern out for him to see.

"Come inside," he said. "I will give you light."

As she entered through the heavy iron doors, she heard Paul's voice again. "Perhaps we can offer some light to you as well, friend."

Lydia could see Paul and Silas, still wearing shackles on their legs, though the chains had come free from their tethers on the wall. A beam from the ceiling of their cell had snapped and fallen in on them. Both men had small cuts and bruises, though most of their injuries were from the flogging.

Two other prisoners sat in the next chamber, which still appeared to be intact. They looked as stunned as Arsene that they had not tried to escape.

"Do any of you know this woman?" the jailer asked, gesturing to Lydia.

"Yes," Silas answered when he finally recognized her in the dim torch light. "She is our dear friend, Lydia. She sells purple in your forum, Arsene."

"Lydia?" Arsene asked. He turned and studied her dusty face. "Are you here to see *these* men?"

She nodded. "I brought them supper." She looked down at her basket. "Though I think it is ruined now. I dropped it in the dirt."

Arsene looked at his prisoners and back to Lydia. "They did not even try to escape when they had the chance. The doors were all wide open."

Lydia smiled and nodded. "I heard them singing."

Arsene continued. "If they had run away, Takis would have ordered my execution. He would not care about the earthquake. I am charged with keeping the prisoners in any circumstance."

"That is just one reason we could not leave here," Paul explained. "You have done no harm to us, and we wish you no ill will."

"How is it that you are happy to be in jail?" Arsene asked. The men from the other cell seemed to ponder the same question. "You were singing, just as she said."

Paul exchanged a quick glance with Silas, and their smiles broadened. "What greater joy is there but to sacrifice for the one who suffered every indignity for my salvation?"

"Who is this you speak of?" Arsene asked.

Lydia grinned and nodded. "Arsene, may I bring some water for you all?"

He nodded and gestured to the small chamber beyond the heavy outer door. Lydia handed the basket of food to Arsene and excused herself to the jailer's quarters. She found a large jar of fresh water and a tray with an empty cup. The earthquake had shaken over everything in the room. It took her a few minutes to find what she needed for the others. She picked up a cloth and wiped out the cup, and then found a basin and another towel. She gathered the things up and returned to the men.

Silas and Arsene worked together to move the fallen timber from the cell while Paul was sharing the small meal with the other prisoners.

"And this man, Jesus," Arsene said, "actually was crucified after a trial in Pilate's court?"

"He was buried as well," Silas answered. "But three days after he died on the cross, Jesus rose from his grave and was seen by many people. He even … I know you will not believe this, but I saw him. He …"

"He … what?" Arsene demanded.

"He … he ascended."

"Ascended? Where?"

"To his home. To his Father. To … Look. He rose to *heaven*. In a cloud." Silas looked intently at Arsene, watching for signs of disbelief. He saw only a man confused, struggling to comprehend.

Paul nodded. "He appeared to me, too. Until that moment I had been an instrument of the Sanhedrin—the

Jewish high council—who saw Jesus and his disciples as a threat. So I pursued Jesus' followers, and when I found them, I had them stoned, flogged and beaten, even put to death. After I saw Jesus, everything changed for me. I had been a man whose only intention was to inflict harm to a believer and a disciple of this Jesus. And now ... Now *I am* a follower of Jesus. I was the greatest of sinners, but after He had told me that He died for my sins, too, I felt the only peace I have ever known."

Arsene leaned in to hear more clearly. "But I am a Greek, not a Jew. If Jesus is the Jewish Messiah, what does that mean to me?"

Paul gestured for everyone to join him inside the prison cell. When all were assembled, he looked at the huge jailer. "My friend, tell me something. Are you at peace?"

The big man looked puzzled before he answered, "What do you mean? We are not at war, so I guess we must be at peace."

Paul smiled despite his wounds and injuries. "What about in your heart, my friend? Do you feel shame or guilt for things you have done? To put it another way, if God appeared before you today and asked you to answer for all the things you did in this life, would your heart be glad in the telling?" Paul asked gently.

"Of course not!" the big man spat out. "I have killed men. And women, even children. I'm not proud of *all* that I've done in my service, but I *am* proud of my service." He ended with too much voice, and Paul sensed his defensiveness.

"If you knew with certainty that God forgave you all that

you have done for which you feel shame, regret or guilt, would you feel differently?"

"Well, of course, I would!" he said defiantly. "But who can offer this forgiveness of which you speak? Where is your God who would grant even me such an unmerited blessing?"

"*My* God is in heaven, but in Jesus the earth beheld the Son of God, walking and living as a mortal man and moving among us as one of us. He has humbled Himself and asked forgiveness on our behalf. All you have to do to receive the gift is abandon your sinful ways and follow Jesus."

Arsene stopped and looked at a distant scene only he could perceive. "I ... see."

Paul continued, "Jesus is not just the Savior of the Jews. He died—He became the sacrifice to cover the sins of all humanity. All anyone must do is believe in Him and offer themselves in obedience."

Lydia poured a cupful of water and then drew enough water in the basin to wash the men's wounds. As she dipped the rag into the bowl, Arsene took the damp cloth from her hand.

"I will tend to their injuries," he said. "These men saved my life. I owe them mine."

Lydia nodded and looked through the basket for any other food that might still be salvageable. Another tremor shook the walls around them. Though this quake was much less severe than the first, everyone gasped and jumped toward the walls at the sudden movement.

Arsene stood and quickly motioned for the group to follow him to the small courtyard outside. He had removed all the prisoners' bindings.

"Stay here. It will be safer for everyone," Arsene said.

A cool breeze danced around them. Another series of small tremors rattled the bars of the jail as well as Lydia's nerves. Everyone in the group shuddered with cold or fear— or both.

When the last of the aftershocks shook loose the lintel over the heavy jail door, Arsene gestured to the marble steps leading up to the road. "Follow me to my house. It will be safer than this place."

Once up to the street, Lydia's eyes began to adjust to the darkness; and the white marble columns that lined the building fronts seemed to glow in the meager moonlight. All around them were familiar buildings in unfamiliar shapes and positions, and the air was heavy with smoke. Arsene's lantern was too weak to shed light on anything beyond its own bronze shell. Nevertheless, he led them the fifty paces behind the jail to his home, where his wife and son stood at the door, weeping but unharmed.

As soon as they saw Arsene, they ran to him and wrapped around his body like a cloak. "We were afraid," his wife said between sobs. "All I could think about was what would happen to you if the prisoners escaped. Did they all get away? Are we to flee as well?"

Arsene rubbed his son's head and kissed his wife. "I am safe. None of the prisoners ran when the doors opened."

A house servant joined them when he heard Arsene's voice, "Thank the gods, you are here," the servant said with an unsteady bow at the neck.

Arsene shook his head again, and Lydia thought she saw the shimmer of tears in his eyes. "Petros, bring fresh water and bandages." When the servant left them, Arsene led the group to the small open-air yard beside his home. His wife brought another lantern and joined them, all the while chanting a prayer of thanks to Poseidon.

Arsene motioned for her to sit next to him. He scooped his son into his lap and said, "There is only one God to thank, Zoe. These men saved my life. They did not run when they had the chance. Instead, they sang songs of praise to their God."

Petros returned with water and clean bandages, as well as oil for the prisoners' wounds. "I will bring something to eat, too," he said.

Lydia followed him back into the house. "If you will show me, I will prepare the food. You should join the others outside."

Petros knit his brows together and tilted his chin in confusion. "You are not a servant. You wear purple and fine linens. You cannot be waiting on others as a common slave."

Lydia smiled and reached for the young man's hand. "You are a faithful friend to this household. Your master values you more than you know. Be at his side now," she urged him. "I believe your master has a gift for you to honor your service to his household."

"A gift?" Petros asked, puzzled. He scurried out the door and into the darkened courtyard.

Lydia found a basket of fruit and a loaf of bread sitting out on the serving table. *This will do*, she thought, and carried them out to the yard, where Paul was telling them about his encounter with Jesus and his healing and baptism.

Zoe and Arsene smiled when she set the food out for

them, and within just a few minutes, the basket was empty, and the bread was gone. Lydia listened as Paul and Silas explained to the family, as well as the other prisoners, about Jesus of Nazareth and how He was God on earth.

"Arsene," Paul began, "at the jail, you asked what you could do to be saved. You need only believe in the Lord Jesus, and you will be saved—all of you."

Arsene stood up and raised his hands to the sky. His thick, muscular arms flexed over his head. "Creator, God, I have sinned against you," he called out into the blackness.

As his words rose from his lips, Lydia saw a warm humility settle over his shoulders. His arms fell to his sides, his knees bent beneath him, and Arsene dropped to his knees. He reached out to take hold of Zoe's foot as he lowered his forehead to the ground.

"I do not deserve to be saved, Lord," he whispered. "But ... please ... I ask ... forgiveness." With that, the big man's torso shook with sobs of grief and shame.

Zoe joined him on the ground. Petros and the other prisoners knelt as well, rubbing the big man's shoulders and back, offering words of comfort and condolence. In time Arsene stopped sobbing, and soon afterward he sat back on his haunches and sent his tear-stained gaze around the circle of family, servant, and prisoners. "Thank you. I feel ... better. But ... I do not understand something."

"What is that?" Silas asked.

"I do not know your Jesus. I have never seen him. How could I receive his forgiveness and comfort when he is not even here?" Arsene was clearly puzzled.

Paul answered, "God allowed Jesus to come to earth to

grant man forgiveness of his sins and eternal life for his soul. Jesus, in turn, empowers his followers to do mighty works in His name. Should you choose to join us, then you, in turn, will be an instrument of God's grace and mercy to others. And if you are speechless at the gift and terrified of the power then you are in the right group." Paul smiled wistfully as he finished the last sentence.

"I? I could never do what you just did. I could never earn the love of God that you all share so generously. I feel as if I have wasted my life... except for them." Arsene nodded toward his family, who were also staring at the ground, touched by Arsene's sincerity.

Paul shook his head. "Get up. God sees your broken hearts, and He will heal them. There is nothing to earn. You have only to believe."

Arsene straightened his back but remained on his knees. "I do believe in Jesus. What comes next?"

Paul was touched by the simplicity of the big man's words, the lack of guile in his face and voice. "The next step is what we call 'baptism.' It is the ceremonial immersion in water which symbolizes the death, burial, and resurrection of our Lord. It represents the cleansing of the soul by God Almighty and a rebirth as a follower of Jesus in God's service. Baptism is available to you if you want it, and to your family and servants if that is their wish." Paul looked at the others. Silas had nothing to add, but the rest looked thoughtful.

Arsene looked at his wife and son. "Normally I would decide such a matter for you, but this time that will not do. This is a decision each of you must make. For myself, I choose baptism and a new path for my life."

"You are my husband, and I will worship the God you worship," Zoe said. "I choose baptism, too." She was looking directly into Arsene's eyes, her own visage open and trusting, shining with a light he had never noticed before.

Arsene looked at his son. "And you, my son? What is your wish?"

"Baptize me, too, Father," the boy said enthusiastically. "I do not want to be left out."

"When can we be baptized as you were?" Arsene asked Paul.

Paul smiled. "As soon as we can find a body of water large enough to hold you, my giant friend."

Silas began to chuckle, and soon everyone was back to their feet. Joy replaced the fear of the evening, and after a short trek to the trough behind Arsene's house, Paul baptized Arsene and his household, as well as the other cellmates.

"Come inside my home, we will all get a little sleep before the sun rises," Arsene said to the others. "I think the ground has stopped shaking for now."

Paul nodded and followed the small exhausted crowd inside. Lydia waited to speak with him at the doorway.

"I must go home now," she whispered. "There are many gathered there praying for you. I need to let them know you were not hurt in the earthquake."

Paul dipped his chin to her with great respect. "Arsene," he said, calling to his new brother. "Lydia needs to return home, and she has no light for her path. Could you lend her a lantern?"

Arsene and Zoe came back to the doorway to thank her

and wish her well. "Please take a lantern—not just a lantern—take Petros with you. He can return tomorrow."

After a few minutes of prayerful goodbyes, Lydia and Petros took the path to her house in the olive grove. The walk back home seemed much shorter than the walk to the jail. She enjoyed talking to the young house servant. She guessed that he was only a year or two younger than Marcus. He spoke with the same excitement about the things he enjoyed. He furrowed his thick black brows at the things he did not understand, just as Marcus often did.

"How did you come to Arsene's home?" Lydia asked Petros.

"I was born to slaves from Troas," he said. "Arsene bought me to help him with his animals. This was before he was married."

Lydia raised her eyebrows. "You must have been very young,"

"I was just a child. Arsene and Zoe treat me as if I am their family. I feel like Thomas is my baby brother." Petros smiled at Lydia.

As they approached her large home, his jaw dropped in wonder. A group stood on her front steps, waiting for her.

Joel called out when he saw her, "The mistress has returned! She has a guest with her."

Petros looked at his traveling companion. "This is your home?"

"Yes," she said. "Please come inside with the others, Petros. We will find you a suitable bed for the night. You must be tired."

Petros nodded as the crowd, now gathering on Lydia's porch, enfolded him and welcomed him into their midst.

Luke offered a prayer of thanksgiving and then asked Lydia to tell the gatherers what had happened during the night.

She began to regale them with every fantastic detail, but even with the drama of the earthquake, several of the listeners started to list with fatigue. She decided to compress the story into a quick summary and invited anyone to ask for a recounting when she was more refreshed.

Timothy thanked all who stayed vigilant in prayer, and within the hour most of the crowd had gone to their own homes for the night.

Lydia intended to rest, but as she continued to tell Luke about Arsene and his family, she became more excited. She crossed her arms tightly as she relived the terrible earthquake and the sight of Arsene as he prepared to take his own life. Her face lit up as she spoke of Zoe and the sweet little boy.

Luke just smiled and listened.

"This is why you travel all over the world?" she asked him.

"Yes," he answered. "I think now that you have tasted this fruit, you will crave even more." He shrugged. "Like Paul, Silas, Timothy and myself."

As the sun peeked over the crest of Mount Orbelos, Lydia yawned. "You sent me to the jail on purpose, I think." She smiled and rubbed her tired eyes.

"All in God's purpose," Luke said through a yawn.

Lydia spent the early morning swinging between the overwhelming excitement of the evening and growing exhaustion from the sleepless night. She prayed for strength to work through her day and thanked God for Marcus's help in the market. She prayed that no one was hurt in the earthquake.

"We will visit the jail this morning and see if there is anything more that can be done for Paul and Silas," Timothy explained as Lydia prepared to leave for the forum. "We will let you know if we need your help."

Lydia nodded and smiled. Her heart soared, but her mind struggled to stay alert.

"Are you all right?" Luke asked her.

"I am well." She pulled her epiblema over the back of her head and fastened it over her hair. "Marcus will help if I need to rest later."

At the sound of his name, Marcus stormed in through the

front door. "No! I will not help you anymore. I am not a bondservant. I am a citizen—a grown man. I will no longer help you and your friends tear down this city."

Lydia took a step back and blinked in dismay. "What are you talking about, Marcus?"

Her cousin growled and stomped to where Timothy and Luke stood. He sneered at them and then whirled around to face Lydia. "Your other two friends have virtually destroyed Calchas' business. He and Ercole will be ruined if they cannot revive Daphne's abilities."

Lydia wanted to roll her eyes. Instead, she faced her cousin and spoke plainly. "Her abilities? She is a child."

"Gifted by Apollo to see the future," he interrupted.

Lydia shook her head. "She is a slave child. Calchas and Ercole fed her laurel leaves—poison—to induce hallucinations. They are poisoning her for their own gain. This certainly is not a gift, not to her."

"You do not understand the marvels of the gods. They grant strength to some, sight to others, beauty, and grace..."

"Marcus, if your gods were so powerful, how then would she have lost the gift at the mere mention of my God?" Lydia took a deep breath.

"Perhaps a trick; maybe they are sorcerers," he replied.

"Why would you say such a thing about men you do not know? They are messengers, that is all. Even if they had a power of their own—even if what you suggest were true—Calchas and Ercole have had their booth for years, and it has always been successful. Their business is far from ruined. Daphne has only been in Philippi for a short time. I doubt ..."

"These men have only been here for a short time, too,"

Marcus spat, gesturing over his shoulder. "Yet they have made a great change in Philippi. You do not know them, either, but you treat them better than your own family." He took several steps toward Lydia and leaned down until his face was mere inches from hers. "Soon these men will move on, and you will have to deal with Calchas and Ercole again. And me," Marcus hissed.

Lydia stood her ground. "You cannot speak to me..." she began. Before she could finish the sentence, Marcus exploded.

"Woman! I will not argue with you. And I will speak to you in any way that appeals to me, now and in the future." Marcus wheeled, stomped off and disappeared into the trees.

Lydia started to tremble with anger and exhaustion. She sank to the cool marble floor and sobbed.

Luke sent Timothy to get Agatha, then he sat at Lydia's side. He reached out, took her hand, and began to pray. "Almighty Jehovah, comfort your daughter with peace and give her strength. She is willing at heart, Lord, but right now her body is weary."

When Luke paused for breath, Lydia poured out her soul. "Lord God, Creator of the universe, I praise You for Your mighty works."

Luke smiled as she shared the prayer.

She continued. "I ask that You use me and my home to bring the good news of the Messiah to this city. I ask that You remove those like Calchas and Ercole who promote idolatry, and soften Marcus's heart to You." She paused, then ended the prayer with a whisper. "And grant me strength."

Luke squeezed her hand as they finished the prayer. As

Lydia raised her gaze to meet his, he brushed away the traces of tears from her cheeks. "What more can I do for you, sister?" he asked.

Lydia nodded. "I feel much better now," she said. "It seems like just a few days ago that Marcus was learning to walk. When he was little, he would to run to me and throw his arms around my neck. After he had lost his parents, we were still close and could speak with kindness about everything. But it has been different lately. Something changed for Marcus, and he has grown resentful and domineering. It is almost as if he sees the old gods of Rome in competition with Jehovah." She looked at the ground, her voice growing softer. "We argue now. All the time. I do not know what to do with him. He never behaved in such a rude manner before. He never spoke so harshly."

"He is still young." Luke shrugged. "I remember when I was seventeen. It was difficult for me to sort facts from the things I only wished were true. I will confess to you ... I gave my mother plenty of reasons to cry."

Lydia laughed. "And see what a kind man you are now?"

Luke shook his head. "This is God's work, certainly not mine."

Agatha and Timothy rushed in and helped Lydia back to her feet. "Mistress, are you alright? What happened?" Agatha asked, holding tightly to Lydia.

"She will be all right," Luke said. He patted Lydia's shoulder. "Marcus exploded again and created an unpleasant scene," Luke explained.

"What was Marcus angry about this time?" Agatha asked.

"The same as usual lately. He is angry that I do not embrace the gods of Rome and that I still believe in the One God of our people. I fear there can be no peace between us until one of us surrenders his convictions," Lydia concluded.

Agatha took a deep breath and held it for several seconds. Her cheeks reddened until she released it with a gasp. "Such a battle being fought in his heart."

Lydia nodded and leaned on her friend. "Exactly right, Agatha. But I believe my God will win."

Agatha shot a doubtful glance to Luke and Timothy, who only smiled back.

"Your mistress is exhausted," Luke explained. "She needs to rest. If she were my patient, then I would tell her to stay home this morning."

Agatha nodded and directed Lydia toward the stairway. "We shall let you get some sleep. I will send Joel to the market to tend your booth until you feel well."

Luke smiled at Lydia. "Sleep will certainly help, Lydia. Your house is in good hands."

After they had reached her room, Lydia reclined on her bed, and Agatha closed the shutters on her window, blocking out the bright sunlight.

"I will check on you in a few hours," Agatha said from the doorway. "Until then, please try to sleep."

Lydia closed her eyes to shut out the swirling images and conversations that she was too tired to resolve. Soon she fell into a disturbed sleep and a series of dreams in which she was being pulled apart by wild dogs. She cried out, but no one could hear her. She tried to run, but her feet would not move. As each dream ended, Lydia would wake for a few seconds. Her tired body would roll over, and soon she would slip back into another nightmare, each more frightening than the last. After what seemed like hours of terror, Lydia finally woke enough to sit up and rub her eyes.

"Lord God, please rescue me from my fears. I know that You are mightier than any demon in my mind. I have seen Your work with my own eyes. I pray that Your hand will protect me. You are my Father, and I am Your child." As she uttered the last phrase, a deep sleep overtook her.

No dreams played in her mind. No more wrestling—just rest.

Two hours later she awoke feeling more rested and hopeful, and with a new determination to understand Marcus and to love him despite his hostility. She combed out her hair and splashed fresh water over her face and neck. She opened her window again and saw that the sun was already beginning its long descent.

She hurried down the stairs, eager for news about Paul and Silas, but the house seemed to be empty. She went to the kitchen, but Phoebe and Mary were nowhere to be found. She crossed the empty courtyard to the stable, but Joel and Eb were not there, either. She searched the downstairs rooms for Agatha, but nobody was home. Lydia went out to the portico to see if something was happening outside, but she saw no one.

"Agatha? Phoebe? Eb? Is anyone here?" she called out, wondering if she might still be dreaming. Nobody answered.

She knocked at the door to the room where her guests were staying, but the door was ajar, and that room was empty, too. Walking farther down the hall, she saw the door to Marcus's room stood open, so she went inside.

The room was empty, but not like the other rooms in her house. Everything was gone. Marcus had taken all his furniture and belongings. There was nothing left.

Lydia stood frozen in the center of the room. She could not move her feet, and no sound would come from her lips. Her heart slammed against her ribs, and her fingers throbbed. She blinked several times, hoping that suddenly the furnishings would return and she would see Marcus sitting on his bed. Tears filled her eyes, and as she blinked, they rolled over her face in a flood. She prayed that this was another nightmare, but somehow, she knew it was real.

Noise from the hall caught her attention, and she could once again move.

"Is anyone here?" she called out again. Her voice sounded weak in her own ears.

"Lydia?"

She heard Timothy's voice from the hallway and ran to meet him.

"What happened?" she wondered.

Timothy reached out for her and led her to the bench in her front room. "Mary found me just now in the forum and asked me to come back and check on you. She said that Marcus had left home and that everyone was looking for him."

"His room is empty," Lydia said with a matching emptiness in her face and voice. "I do not know where he has gone."

"I know," he said. "Luke is with Paul and Silas. Your

magistrate discovered that they were Roman citizens, and now he is trying to get them out of town quietly. If word reached Rome that Takis had two Roman citizens flogged and imprisoned without a trial, there would be severe trouble for him."

Lydia struggled to process Timothy's words. "You cannot leave now. I need your help. Marcus is gone."

Timothy nodded. "Do not worry. I will stay with you. Paul and Silas will not go quietly. We will not leave you in this kind of distress. We will find Marcus, I assure you."

Lydia looked into Timothy's caring eyes. He was not very much older than Marcus was, but he seemed a great deal more disciplined and mature.

"Thank you, Timothy," she said. "Where are the others?"

"Looking for Marcus. They are all over town. Joel and Eb closed your booth, and they are searching the palaestra and the temples." Timothy took a deep breath. "Phoebe, Agatha and Mary are asking friends if they know where he might be."

"What about Calchas and Ercole?" she asked.

Timothy thought for a second. "I saw Calchas in his booth. I did not see Ercole."

Lydia stood and smoothed her peplos with the palms of her hands. She knew what she needed to do. "I must go. I think I know where Marcus is."

"I will go with you." He stood at her side and led her toward the door. "Just in case we find him."

Lydia nodded. She was glad for the company. She wrapped her epiblema around her shoulders and was ready for her task.

"We will first go to Ercole's house. Marcus looks up to him. If Marcus is not there, then we can find his friend, Epaphroditus. They have been close since they were children, but he still lives with his mother and father. If Marcus has gone to Epaphroditus' home, then I do not think he would have taken his bed." Lydia stood at the gate of her courtyard and considered the city that spread out in front of her. "Perhaps he has just taken his things to scare me. Maybe he will return tonight." She took a deep breath, looked at Timothy, and said, "Come. Let us go now."

Timothy grimaced, wishing she were right about Marcus but fearful that she was a prisoner of her own hope. Lydia nodded, recognizing that he doubted a resolution before nightfall. She walked on, occasionally looking at Timothy and wishing that she had raised Marcus to be more like him.

"I suppose your family is proud of you and your work," she said.

"Yes," he said, "I think they are. But they are also aware of the perils Rome can visit on those of us who follow Jesus."

"How did you come to be a follower?" Lydia asked.

"My mother and grandmother began teaching me about Jesus when I was still a child. They saw Jesus and heard him speak when they were in Jerusalem. Mother talked about how Jesus fulfilled the prophecies of ancient times, the prophecies that foretold a Messiah."

Lydia shrugged her shoulders as she walked. "You are Greek. How did you come to know about the prophecies of the Messiah?"

Timothy sighed. "I am Greek, but I studied the Torah with my grandfather. My mother and grandmother studied with us. After their experience with Jesus, they told me that they just *knew*."

"I felt the same way when I heard you all speak at the river. I wish I had seen Jesus," Lydia said. At the corner of the forum, Lydia gestured to a block of homes to her right. "This way."

Timothy looked up at the darkening sky. "The day is almost done. If he is not here, then I think we should return to your home and search more tomorrow."

"Then let him be here. I believe that it is this one." Lydia nodded as they reached Ercole's home. It had not suffered much damage from the earthquake. The house was not big, but it was finished with remarkable artisanship. On the front portico, detailed capitals topped four marble columns that were linked together with carved stone arches.

Lydia took a deep breath and rapped on the door. A few seconds had passed before a young servant boy answered the door. Lydia raised her eyebrows at the appearance of the child. His eyes were red and swollen, and his cheeks looked flushed.

Lydia peered inside over the boy's head but could see nothing except the vague outline of a dim room. The shutters were all closed, and a single lamp provided the only source of light.

"Are you all right?" she asked.

"Yes, Miss," he answered. "Are you here to see Ercole?"

"Yes, I am. Is he here?"

He hesitated and looked back over his shoulder. "I will ask." He shut the door.

Timothy looked around them. "So, is he going to ask his

master if his master will admit if he's home? That seems strange to me."

Lydia nodded. She, too, felt as if something was wrong. She waited for a few more seconds and then knocked again.

This time Ercole opened the door. His appearance was that of a wild man. His eyes looked wide and black, red-rimmed and bloodshot, and his face was pale. He wore a short toga wrapped loosely at one shoulder, and his torso was damp with sweat. "Oh. It's you."

Lydia stared at him in dismay. "Ercole, are you ill?"

He shook his head and stepped out on the portico, closing his door behind him. "No, Lydia. I am as well as anyone could expect. Business has been slow today. People are cleaning up after the quake. And nobody wants to visit our booth since our seer has lost her sight. You should know that."

Lydia ignored the jab. "I am looking for Marcus. Is he here?"

Ercole crossed his arms over his chest. "Marcus is no longer a child, Lydia. He can go where he chooses."

Now Lydia knew Marcus was in there. "Of course, you are correct," she said, surrendering the point. "Would you ask Marcus if he chooses to come to the door and speak with me?"

"Well, now, I do not know. Who told you Marcus was here?" he asked in a dismissive tone. He shifted his feet from side to side.

Lydia took a deep breath and recognized the smell of the incense that had made her sick last week. She squinted and took an assertive step toward Ercole. "You did. Would you please send for Marcus now? I need to speak with him."

"He is in no mood for you," he said, stepping backward and bumping his shoulders against his door.

"And how would you know that, Ercole?" Lydia asked without a hint of condescension or resentment. Ercole stood there, speechless, staring at Lydia. "Marcus," Lydia called loudly, hoping he could hear her through the door. "I must speak with you. Right now, right here."

The door opened again, and Marcus stepped out. His hair was tangled, and his face looked sickly. Like Ercole, his eyes were red and puffy, and perspiration covered his bare chest.

"You cannot order me about any longer." His words slurred together, and he swayed as he spoke. "I am my own citizen. Go home, Lydia."

Her heart broke as she stared at her cousin. With every ounce of her being, she wanted to hold him in her arms while she carefully and repeatedly kicked his backside. "Please, Marcus, listen to me. You are my kinsman, and I love you. There is no harm I would wish on you even if I could. I do not want to remake you when God is satisfied with you as you are, but neither do I want to see you cast out of our home and living like a beggar."

"This is my home now," Marcus said. "I will be working for Calchas from now on. We are trying to help Daphne regain her sight."

Lydia listened to him but had to work to focus on what he was saying. "Is Daphne well?" she asked.

Marcus hissed. "Still interested in everybody else more than me?" He gestured to the door. "Ercole and I are going back inside. You should go home and take care of your friends."

Lydia shook her head and appealed to him. "Marcus ..." But he ignored her and turned away. Ercole shrugged and followed Marcus into the house, leaving Lydia and Timothy alone.

Timothy took her hand and helped her down the steps.

Lydia stifled her sobs as they headed back to the house. Timothy held her arm to keep her steady. They made the short walk in silence.

She sniffed when they reached the edge of the olive grove, and she saw the crowd gathered on her front steps. "At least I know where he is," she finally whispered to Timothy. "Thank you for your company."

As she reached her house, the congregation surrounded her, and Paul stepped forward.

She felt a weight of worry lift from her heart when she realized that both Paul and Silas were safe and free. Silas began a song of praise, and Paul and Luke stationed themselves on either side of Lydia.

As she listened to the songs and prayers, Lydia's knees became weak, and she collapsed in the center of the crowd. Luke picked her up and carried her inside.

"Sit down and try to breathe slowly," Luke advised. He put the back of his hand to her forehead. "No fever. That is important."

"We found Marcus," she said. "We need to pray."

Luke smiled and nodded. "You have been a ship in a storm today. Up and down and battered by the waves. You go and rest. We will pray."

CHAPTER

ELEVEN

Lydia awoke to the sound of a man singing. It took her several seconds to clear her head enough to realize that it was not Simeon but Silas who was ringing out a psalm of praise. She smiled and yawned, determined to make this day better than yesterday.

She dressed and twisted her hair into a braid. Looking into her mirror, she forced a smile and dusted some pearl powder over her cheeks. Her eyes still felt puffy from tears, but she felt rested.

"Did you sleep soundly?" Agatha asked, bringing Lydia a cup of fresh water.

"Yes." She squeezed Agatha's hand. "I heard Silas singing this morning. Are they well?"

"Their wounds are mending, and they are working on some kind of plan for the week. All four men have been talking and singing since very early this morning." Agatha helped to straighten the folds of Lydia's dress across the back. "Timothy told the others about how you found Marcus. They talked about what you might need and then prayed for a long time."

Lydia nodded. "It is such a blessing to have them all here. Not just in Philippi, but here in our home, too."

Agatha pressed her lips together tightly and turned her focus to the window. Lydia sensed there was something amiss. "What is it, Agatha?"

Agatha shook her head and shrugged. "I cannot be sure. The men have not mentioned anything specifically, but after their prayers, Timothy went out for a time. When he returned, I heard him say something about traveling weather."

Lydia frowned as her mind jumped from one worry to another. "I do not want them to leave," she said without hesitation. "They have only just started their work here. Have we failed them so terribly that they would give up?"

Agatha shook her head quickly. "Do not worry about that yet. Perhaps I misheard their words. Maybe they were speaking more about the type of weather than of traveling."

Lydia sighed and quickly drank the cup of water. "I will talk to them right away."

She hurried downstairs to find that all four of her guests were out already. Phoebe, Mary, and Korinna worked in the garden, enjoying the cool of the morning, and Joel and Eb were both at the stable.

Lydia checked in Marcus's bedroom, but it remained empty. Her mind again clouded with worries about her guests departing soon, about Marcus's leaving, about how to bring him back home, and about how to take care of her business without anyone to help her. She needed assurance. She needed strength. She needed hope.

"I must get to the market," she told Agatha. "I will be alone today."

Agatha nodded. "I will bring you something to eat soon. Korinna and I want to go through some of your new merchandise and select some things for embellishment." She helped Lydia pin her scarf over her hair. "Do not fret about what to do."

"I was not fretting." Lydia raised her brows and shook her head.

"Yes, you were," Agatha said with a smile. "But worrying will not help matters."

Lydia smiled despite herself. "Will you be coming to the shop soon?"

"Yes." Agatha nodded. "Go now, and be careful."

Lydia hurried to her booth, embarrassed to be arriving at the square so late in the morning. As she saw others just opening their shops, too, she remembered that the sun was higher in the sky because of the change in seasons.

Lydia quickly raised her awning and said her morning prayers, asking God to pour out His mercy on Marcus, Daphne, and her guests. She busied herself with making sure her stock was in place around her shop after the disturbance of the earthquake. She had no customers yet—the whole forum was still quiet—so Lydia took a seat at the front of her booth and tried to relax.

She suddenly heard a loud crash from Calchas' shop. She jumped up and ran to see what happened. Daphne lay on the ground sobbing, with a table's worth of brass bowls upset all around her. Calchas stood a few feet away, his arms crossed over his puffed-up chest. His face looked red and twisted in anger. Ercole and Marcus both waited at the back of the booth, flinching from Calchas' wrath.

"What happened?" Lydia heard herself say as she stepped between Calchas and Daphne.

"I am ruined!" Calchas roared. "She cannot see the future anymore!" He thrust his hands toward Daphne as if she were nothing more than rubbish on the floor. "Ercole and Marcus have done everything they can to make her see, but now the herbs and potions only make her sick. She will probably die before they can heal her." Calchas kicked in her direction, and Lydia took Daphne's arm and backed toward the side of the stall.

Looking down at the girl, Lydia could see that she was pale. Not just fair-skinned, but white and sickly. Her green eyes looked dull, with dark gray circles beneath them. Daphne's whole body trembled. "There is nothing wrong with her that cannot be cured with a proper diet, some rest, and ..." she looked pointedly at Marcus, "... a safe home." She held out her arms to shield the girl from anything Calchas might decide to throw.

"She is no use to me," Calchas spat at Lydia. "Just being here in this booth makes her ill. By Zeus, just having her here is making me sick, too. I will hand her over to Takis to be punished."

Lydia dropped to her knees to guard the child. "She has done nothing wrong!" she insisted. "You cannot have her punished."

Calchas bent at his waist and pushed his face down to

within inches of Lydia's. "She is my property. I can do with her as I wish. If I ask Takis to have her stoned in the theater for my own entertainment, no one can stop me." He looked at Lydia with disgust, and his next words were intended to cut her heart out. "Not even a man."

Lydia knew this was true. Her heart slammed in her chest as she drew a long deep breath. Her lungs filled with the smell of Calchas' sweat and the heavy odor of the spices all around her.

"Let me buy her from you," she said. Her heart felt bold as the words spilled into the tense air between them. "You spent a year's profit on her. Let me redeem your loss."

Calchas scoffed. "That is not enough, now. It is much more than her purchase price, you know. I have invested in her care—her nourishment, her lodging, her clothes—and she has been a great expense to me, over and above what I had to spend to acquire her in the first place."

"I will pay a year and a half's profit for her," Lydia blurted out. Ercole and Marcus stepped closer to see Calchas' reaction to the offer.

Calchas stopped for a moment, apparently performing complex calculations. "A year and a half of your profit, or a year and a half of my profit?"

"I meant a year and a half of my profit," Lydia answered without flinching.

Calchas scoffed. "Your profit? Laughable. It would have to be a year and a half of my profit," he insisted.

"And how much was your profit last year, Calchas?" she asked innocently.

"Sixty drachmas," he pronounced proudly.

"So for a year and a half, you would expect 90 drachmas?" Lydia asked.

"Yes."

"Done," she agreed.

"Wait! How much was your profit last year?" Calchas realized he had left himself exposed.

"Three hundred drachmas," she stated, "but I am happy to meet your terms."

Calchas blanched, realizing that in his arrogance, he had forfeited a small fortune, but his raging mind could not find a way out. He decided to try a different approach. "It is not just the money, Lydia," Calchas said, flexing his fingers in front of her face. "You above all understand how important one's reputation is in a city like Philippi. It will take me a long time to rebuild my position in the marketplace. Such an enormous effort must also be compensated."

Lydia relaxed her shoulders and let her hand rest on Daphne's ankle. She felt the trembling fade under her touch. She stared up at Calchas' red face and nodded. "I'm afraid that redeeming your reputation will be at your own expense." Lydia rose to her feet and growled at her rival. "Just so there is no misunderstanding, my offer is for a healthy, unharmed girl. If she is beaten or hurt in any way, you will get nothing."

"Alright!" Calchas roared. "Bargaining with you is like breaking boulders with a stylus." He turned back to bare his teeth at Lydia as if he had planned the whole exchange from the beginning. "Take the little dog from my sight, and bring me my silver before sundown."

Calchas dismissed Lydia and Daphne with a flick of his

wrist, and without another word, Lydia helped the girl to her feet and led her out of Calchas' fetid stall.

When the two women returned to Lydia's booth, they found Agatha walking up with a basket of food.

"Agatha, take care of the shop for me, and feed her," she instructed her maidservant. "Her name is Daphne. Keep her in the back, and make sure that nobody bothers her—especially Calchas or Ercole. She needs to rest." Lydia straightened her peplos and epiblema and took a deep breath for courage. "I must go back to the house, but I will not be long."

Agatha nodded and quickly helped Daphne recline onto the small pallet in the back of the booth. As she spread out the meal for the child, she called to Lydia, "It is good that you go back to the house. I passed Takis on the road here."

Lydia hurried away. As soon as she was out of sight of the market, she quickened her pace, and once under cover of the olive grove, she ran. She slowed only when her house came into view. Two of Takis' soldiers and a white horse waited on her front steps.

The men barely acknowledged her presence as she started up the steps. She could hear men's voices arguing from within the house. She hesitated before opening the door, whispering a quick prayer. "Lord, be over my home."

She walked in on a small crowd. Takis, Paul, Silas, Luke, Timothy, and Joel stood in the main hall. Each man maintained a defensive posture.

"You do not understand the position you have put me in," Takis shouted. "If you had only told someone..."

Paul raised his hand to interrupt. "And when might I

have offered this information? While your men were strip-ping my tunic from my back or while they were flogging us?"

Silas addressed Takis with narrowed eyes as he let a calm smile settle on his face. "And you do not seem like the type of man who enjoys being publicly embarrassed."

Takis dropped his gaze to the marble floor and took a deep breath. Lydia took advantage of the pause to step into the men's conversation, taking her place between Luke and Joel.

"Takis, what brings you to my house?" she asked.

All six of the men turned to face her with shocked expressions. Even Joel blinked at her audacity.

Takis raised his chin and chuffed. "I have come," he said, forcing an air of authority, "to reason with your house guests."

As soon as Takis acknowledged her position, she knew she had the upper hand. "That should be easy enough without a troop of soldiers," Lydia replied. "My guests are reasonable men."

Takis lashed out at the woman's effrontery. "I find them very unreasonable."

"And tell me, Takis, in what ways do you find them unreasonable?"

Paul and Luke exchanged stifled grins. Silas let his smile burst wide, while Timothy's brows rose as high as his fore-head would allow. Joel only looked at his feet.

Takis clasped his hands together behind his back and slowly let his gaze meet Lydia's. "Woman, you forget your place. But since this is your home and these men are your guests, I will answer. Your friends, Paul and Silas, failed to tell me that they were Roman citizens."

Lydia nodded, fully understanding Takis' predicament. "I see. You humiliated, flogged and jailed two citizens without a hearing, stripping them of their Roman rights." She sighed as if she felt sympathy for the man. "Who do you think will treat you more harshly, Rome—when your superiors hear of this—or Calchas when he discovers that you have set them free?"

Takis looked up to the high ceilings of the great hall. "I have come to ask them to leave Philippi quietly." He squared his jaw as he surveyed the other men. "It really would be best for everyone involved."

"Joel," Lydia murmured. "Please bring something for Takis to drink. He seems thirsty. And for the others, as well," she added.

Joel nodded and quickly disappeared. Lydia gestured to the couches by the windows. "Please, gentlemen, sit and discuss these matters more comfortably."

The men could not help but comply with her request. She waited for them to sit first, and then took the seat closest to Takis.

Paul took a deep breath. "Do you really believe it is in our best interest to disappear into the night?"

Takis nodded, but nobody in the room believed him, least of all himself. "With the earthquake, you might have escaped."

"We could have done so if we had wished," Silas said.

"And why did you not?" Takis asked.

"For the same reason we will not allow you to tell your

citizens that we escaped your jail now. It would mean Arsene's execution," Paul answered.

"Not necessarily," Takis held out his hand to plead his argument.

Luke tilted his forehead toward Takis. "You honestly believe that Calchas would not demand Arsene's death?"

Takis shrugged. "Perhaps you do not understand. You *must* leave Philippi today. Calchas is a very powerful man. He has friends throughout the empire; but, even more important, he has many friends here. Powerful friends. If you decide to stay, then he will have you killed. There are men in this town who will do anything for him. Even murder."

Timothy looked to his friends. Lydia watched Paul and Silas as they maintained calm expressions in the face of so bald a threat.

Joel brought in an amphora of watered wine, poured out cups for everyone, and then retreated again to another room. Lydia was confident that Joel waited just out of view, listening carefully for her call.

She smiled as the men all took sips of wine. "Takis, I am sure that your soldiers are perfectly capable of keeping my guests safe."

Takis shot her a worried look. "My soldiers are no less desperate than any other man in Philippi."

His words hit her like a hand slap. She blinked, struggling to suppress a shocked reaction. "They..." She could not finish her thought aloud.

Paul set his cup on the table and turned his palms upward. "If we left as you asked, and if Calchas' friends are everywhere," he said, gesturing around him, "then none of us would be safe anywhere. No, we will not slip into the darkness."

Takis spat out a frustrated gasp. Before he could say another word, Lydia held up her hands, hoping to soften his stance.

"Wait, Takis. Your mistake before was acting without hearing these men. Do not make the same error again. Let them speak," she urged.

Luke nodded and turned to Paul, who closed his eyes for a second and then began. "We will leave Philippi."

Lydia's heart began to race. This was not what she wanted to hear. Takis was the one in the wrong, not Paul and the others. She resisted the urge to shake her head and plead for them to stay. *Do not leave me. My faith is still weak,* she thought.

Takis straightened his shoulders and smiled. "You see reason."

Paul nodded. "But we will not go under cover of darkness. You and your men will escort us from the city, and you will explain your error to the town."

Takis began to mutter, but Paul continued. "You will make sure that Arsene does not suffer any punishment for his part in your error, and you will make it clear to every Philippian that we, as Roman citizens under your protection, are not to be followed or molested. By anyone."

Takis tightened his lips and flexed his jaw. Lydia could tell that he did not want to accept these terms, but it was evident to her that he had little choice. Apparently, Takis came to the same conclusion.

Silas spoke up before Takis could make a sound. "We will

leave your proud city after we have had a good fill of food and fellowship with the friends we have made here. We will enjoy one last night's rest here in Lydia's home, and then we will leave tomorrow morning."

Paul smiled and nodded. "That would not be too much to ask ... even if we were asking."

Everyone waited for Takis' response. He took another sip of wine and then looked at the ceiling as if the solution to all of his problems was carved in the plaster above. When he lowered his chin, he took a deep breath before speaking. "And then you all will leave?"

Lydia's heart ached as she waited for Paul's answer. How could she deal with Marcus without them? What would happen to Daphne? The gatherings? She still needed them.

Paul nodded to Takis. "Silas and I will leave, and we will take young Timothy with us. Our friend Luke will remain here for a time."

A light sparked in Lydia's heart. Her worries faded again. "Thank you, Lord," she whispered.

"I think all of you should go," Takis insisted.

Lydia cleared her throat. "Luke is a doctor, Takis. Philippi needs a good physician. Think of all the people he could treat. Think of the lives he could save. If you asked him to stay here, then these people would owe their good health to you."

Takis looked at Lydia with a mix of fury and admiration. He conceded. "Luke," he began, regarding the doctor, "on behalf of Rome, I invite you to stay in Philippi and provide care for our citizens."

Luke smiled at Lydia and nodded to Takis. "I would be honored."

Takis stood, and the other men joined him. Lydia remained seated, unsure that she could stay upright after that exchange. Her heart pounded, and within her peplos, her whole body shook.

The men clasped each other's wrists in agreement.

"My guard and I will come for you tomorrow morning," Takis announced.

"We will be ready," Paul said.

Takis stormed out.

Lydia listened as the horse and soldiers carried Takis back to his office in the forum. She closed her eyes tightly, trying to stop the panic that was welling up inside her from bursting forth in a storm of tears and screams. The men returned to her side and hugged her shoulders.

"I have never seen a woman, or anyone for that matter, deal with a magistrate so shrewdly," Silas said, "or so forcefully. I should like to have you at my side when I appear before Caesar."

"Thank you for standing up for us," Paul added. "You may have placed yourself in danger by doing so, but we offer your name to God in blessing."

"Takis cannot do anything to me," she said. "He is afraid of Calchas, but I am not." Her thoughts jumped back to Daphne. "I apologize for my lack of hospitality, but I must get back to my booth." She stood and called out to Joel, who stepped into the room immediately. Lydia commanded him, "Prepare a feast for tonight's gathering. Send out the word that it will be our friends' last night with us."

Joel nodded and disappeared. Lydia squeezed the hands of the other men. "I have much to do before you go. Stay here and rest. I will be back as soon as I can."

Lydia hurried upstairs to where she kept her earnings. She counted out enough silver coins to redeem Daphne and then dropped them into a kidskin pouch dyed in the deepest purple that Simeon had ever managed to create. The bag was finished with golden cords that she tied securely and fixed at her waist, underneath her cloak. Lydia took another pouch from her box and filled it with silver coins and the gold bracelets she had taken with her to the prison. After closing the second purse, she returned it to the box and locked everything away.

Luke waited for her at the foot of the stairs. "May I accompany you to your shop?" he asked.

"Yes, of course," she said. Her voice shook more than she expected.

Luke and Lydia walked through the trees in silence. She tried to breathe evenly, but as her thoughts flitted around her mind like birds building a nest, she found herself first holding her breath and then gasping, each in turn.

As they reached the clearing, Luke took her arm gently, and she turned to face him. "You showed real courage," he said.

His hands were warm on her arms. She wanted to lean against his shoulder and cry, but she had too much to do. She feared that if she allowed herself a few tears, then she would not be able to stop.

"I did not want you to leave," she whispered. "Any of you."

Luke smiled. "When the others go, would you like me to find another place to stay?" he asked. "I do not want anyone to question your propriety."

Lydia shook her head. "I cannot bear to have you all leave my home. We can speak about this later."

Luke nodded and started to walk again but then paused, and he gazed into Lydia's eyes. "You amaze me," he whispered. "You have a beautiful spirit."

Lydia tried to speak, but no words could escape her lips. She stared up at this man and wondered if she would ever have the strength to let him leave her. She knew that one day he surely must. She prayed that when that day came, she would have the courage to let him go.

"I must go to see Calchas," she said, pulling back toward the forum.

"You should not be the one to tell him about this," Luke said. "He may not take it well."

"I will not mention any of this to him. I have other business with Calchas. I have bought..." she ran out of breath as she spoke.

Luke held out his hand and took hers. "You bought something from him?"

She nodded as they continued their way into the marketplace. "Not some*thing*, some*one*. I purchased Daphne from him." She looked up at his face, unsure of how he might react.

He took both of her hands in his. "Beautiful spirit," he repeated with a smile. "Your faith is remarkable."

"Is this faith?" she asked. "I just cannot allow that man to misuse and discard the poor child any longer."

"You love her. You cannot help it."

"It is no more than what any other would do."

Luke shook his head. "Nobody else would do this for her. You are saving a slave's life. It is everything." Luke's eyes filled with tears. "To Daphne it is everything."

"But is it faith?" Lydia asked. It took every ounce of her resolve not to throw herself into Luke's arms. She held his hands tightly.

"Love is the greatest part of faith."

Lydia swallowed hard and turned her face toward the forum to prevent herself from saying anything she might wish back. "I know he can be a dangerous man, and he is a tough negotiator, but I could not allow his abuse to continue."

Luke nodded as they arrived at the shop.

Lydia gestured to the back of her booth. "She is in there with Agatha. I would appreciate it if you would see to her condition."

"Of course." Luke released her hand and went back to sit with Daphne, and Lydia went next door to conduct her business.

"Calchas, I have your money," she announced. She scanned the shop, looking for Marcus, but the contrast of entering the dark booth from the bright sunlight made it difficult to see.

"I like that you did not wait until the last minute to take care of business," Calchas' voice boomed from his chair by the front entrance.

She stepped inside and allowed her eyes to adjust. The smell of the spices stung at her nose, but she refused to let them make her sick. "I want to finish our business before you change your mind."

He coughed. "You know, Lydia, that I am an honest businessman. I do not let my whims guide my decisions."

Lydia nodded. "I know you well, Calchas." She reached for the pouch fastened at her side. "I want to thank you for allowing me to purchase your slave. I know how long you waited for her, and I know how this situation has upset you."

"Yes," he said. He puffed up his chest to match the breadth of his belly. "I am ready to be done with this tribulation."

Tribulation? Lydia nearly gasped at the man's self-pity. She held the bag of silver in her hands, fingering the soft leather and remembering how proud Simeon had been when he achieved the depth of color on the leather. She wished he were with her.

"That is why I brought your payment in this," she said, holding out the pouch to him.

Calchas' eyes seemed to glow with pleasure as he took the bag in hand. Ercole and Marcus stepped into view to see what she brought.

"That was Simeon's," Marcus said, recognizing the bag.

"I remember how your husband treasured this piece," Calchas said, admiring the bag. He almost seemed to forget that it held a year and a half's worth of silver.

"It was his most prized possession," Lydia replied. "I hoped that you might accept it as a peace offering between my household and yours."

Calchas softened his stare and grinned. "My dear Lydia, we are friends. I hold no ill will against you or any member of your household. As such, I will accept this gift and treasure it as your husband did."

Lydia nodded and gestured to Marcus and Ercole. "They have witnessed our exchange."

"Yes, yes," Calchas said. "Our transaction is settled."

Lydia dipped her chin to Calchas and then turned and repeated the nod to Marcus and Ercole. "Thank you." She started to leave, but when she saw Marcus's grin, she decided to test her courage again. "May I ask a favor?"

Calchas raised his brow. "What may I grant you, my friend?"

Lydia bowed her head once more. "May I speak with Marcus for a moment?"

Calchas waved his hand in the air as if Lydia was wasting his time with the question. "Yes, yes, but speak in your own booth. I would not want you to disturb my customers."

Lydia scanned the booth. Besides her and the three men, the shop was empty. She decided it would be rude to laugh, so she motioned to Marcus and led the way to the front of her shop.

"What do you want from me, Lydia?" Marcus had asked before she had the chance to speak.

"I thought that, since the situation was settled between Calchas and me, you might come back home."

Marcus shook his head. "I did not leave your house because of what happened to Daphne." He threw a cold stare at her.

Lydia bit her lip, wondering if she made a mistake in talking with him. "Then I do not understand."

"You do not understand why because you do not understand me."

"Help me to understand, Marcus," Lydia pleaded.

Marcus shook his head. "As long as you consider strangers more important to you than me, you will never understand."

Lydia reached out for his hands, but he pulled away and stepped back toward Calchas. "Marcus, please listen. You are the most important person in my life."

Marcus scoffed. "No. You cannot convince me of that after what you just paid for a slave girl."

Lydia knit her brows and shook her head. "You think that I would give less for you? I would give my life for you."

Marcus turned and walked away. "If only you would."

As she watched him disappear into the booth next door, all she could think of was how she could convince him to come home. *Jehovah God, I cannot do this. I do not know what to say to bring him to You. I am not strong enough or good enough or... I am not enough to save him, Lord.*

CHAPTER

TWELVE

Lydia greeted her friends as they arrived for nightly prayers. The crowd was larger than it had been before, probably because Agatha had spread the word of an important announcement. Lydia had requested that everyone attending bring a few pieces of silver or whatever they had to spare.

Though nobody knew why she might ask for money, they knew Lydia to be fair in her financial dealings; and her guests brought what they could. She discreetly gathered the money in a small chest by the door and directed the worshippers into the courtyard.

When the last person arrived, Lydia shut the door and sighed. She did not want her friends to leave, but she was becoming more and more aware of how dangerous this city could be for them. She put the money chest away and instructed her household staff to join the gathering.

Silas was already leading the group in praise, and Luke motioned for her to join him at the edge of the courtyard.

"Dear friends," Paul began when the song was over. "You have welcomed us with warm embraces, and you received our message with open hearts."

Lydia tried to listen to his message, but the thought of tomorrow's departure weighed heavily on her mind. As Paul began to talk about singing in the jail and the earthquake, Lydia started to cry.

Korinna sat at the other end of the bench, and when she saw Lydia's tears, she reached out for her hand. "You must have been frightened," Korinna whispered.

Lydia nodded, realizing that the others around her thought the tears were brought on by Paul's story. *Only Luke understands*, she thought. She glanced up at him, making eye contact.

"I think I should look in on Daphne," she murmured into Luke's ear. "She is resting."

Luke caught her arm before she could stand. "No, she is with us." He pointed to the girl at Paul's feet. "She is over there."

Lydia raised her brows. The sight of Daphne's smile cheered her. She watched for a few minutes as Daphne leaned forward, as if not to miss a single word. Lydia looked around her and saw that every person in the courtyard held the same attentive expression. As Paul spoke of Arsene drawing his sword, the others appeared worried. When he talked about going to the jailer's house and baptizing his family, a halo of joy settled over the group.

In all her busyness, Lydia had let the wonder slip away.

She had taken care of all the details of the evening and then utterly forgotten about the reason she was here. Her heart felt broken, but this time the tears did not come. Instead, a small voice tugged at her mind. *Listen...*

She took a deep breath and focused. Paul began telling the group about all the places he had been because of the message of Jesus. He told them about his desire to go to Rome and Spain. Lydia imagined how difficult and dangerous the journey to Rome might be. Looking at Paul and Silas, she did not see fear or anxiety in their faces. She saw only joy.

Looking at Timothy, she saw something more. She saw the way he beamed, admiring the older men's courage and maturity. She watched his face and knew that he longed to have such a grasp of the message of Jesus that it struck out the fear of persecution. She knew that he wanted to be able to speak as boldly and easily as they did. *He wants to grow to be like them*, she thought. She had seen a similar look before on Marcus's face when he would watch Simeon work.

How she wished for Marcus to be with them now.

Paul concluded his message with the announcement that he, Silas, and Timothy would be leaving Philippi in the morning. Several people moaned and gasped at the news. They vocalized the aches of Lydia's heart. Now, as she watched and listened, Lydia felt at peace with their departure.

She felt not an impending loss but a new opportunity to serve, instead. As the congregation murmured, Silas began another song; and Luke turned to Lydia, gesturing toward the door. She stood with him and followed him inside.

"I will have Agatha and Phoebe bring out the meal," Lydia said.

"I can help," Luke said with a nod. "It helps me to be doing something. I already miss Paul, Silas, and Timothy, for I know the path they walk. Helping with dinner is just what the physician ordered." Lydia whipped her head around, saw the twinkle in Luke's eyes and his stoic sobriety everywhere else, and burst into laughter. When she had command of herself, she bowed and said, "Then please come with me, sir, and I will lead you to your treatment." He followed Lydia into the kitchen.

Agatha had seen them leave the courtyard, and she was already preparing to serve. Phoebe, Mary, and Korinna joined them shortly. Within minutes the guests were enjoying their last night of fellowship with the travelers. Paul, Silas, and Timothy visited with every person and encouraged each one to continue meeting and sharing the good news of Jesus with everyone they knew.

"Luke will remain in Philippi until the Lord calls him to another place. I ask that you all take care of him when we have gone. He has been a great encouragement to me. He will need your support, too." Paul motioned to Luke to stand. "If you show him the same love as you have offered me, he will always be filled to overflowing."

Luke stood for a second and raised his hand. "May I offer a prayer for your journey, brother?"

Paul nodded, and the crowd grew quiet.

Luke began, "Oh Father in Heaven, we praise Your holy name and offer thanks for Your blessings and mercy, Lord," he paused, and Lydia could hear the emotion in his voice. "I pray that You will go before our brothers, and make smooth their paths. Protect them in their travels, and bring them back to Your church here in Philippi if that is Your will." His voice cracked, and Lydia could hear others around her sobbing.

As Luke finished his prayer, the room boomed with a collective, "Amen," and Silas began another song. Everyone listened as his usually deep voice struggled to maintain a melody. Lydia retreated inside to fetch the small chest of money.

Luke followed her in. "What is wrong?"

"Nothing," she replied, showing him the box. "I have a gift for the others. We all collected some money to make their journey easier." She opened the box for Luke to see inside.

His eyes widened at the sight of the silver. "You did this?"

"Not alone," she gestured to the gathering. "Everybody brought something."

"Everybody," Luke echoed. "Hmm! You know, Lydia, I have traveled widely both to the east and to the west, usually with companions but often alone, and I have known other cities and gatherings in which generosity was much on display. Always there is someone, some single person, whose special gift to this world is to bless others by bringing bounty to need. No place I have ever visited can equal such a level of generosity as you have shown to us." Luke patted his hand over his heart. "I am blessed to be staying."

Lydia smiled and led him back to the courtyard. She motioned for Silas and Timothy to join Paul in the center of the group. As she held out the box to them, the yard filled with chatter.

"We have taken a collection for the three of you. We hope this will help as you travel. And if you find others who are in need along the way, please serve them as you see best." Lydia handed the box over, and Paul opened it. His jaw dropped, and he reached out to Silas and Timothy, pulling them to look inside. They stared in disbelief, first one and then the other collapsing to his knees, reaching out to gently touch the coins to rule out a mirage.

"This is a great gift you send with us," Silas said, recovering his voice. "Philippi has blessed us every day."

Timothy nodded. "We will make your generosity known wherever we go."

Paul could not speak. After handing the chest to Silas, he went from one person to the next, kissing their cheeks and speaking blessings over them. "This is God's church. You are God's hands and feet. You are His saints, and you carry His word wherever you go. With your gifts, we can surely go into the whole world with the news of Jesus."

The people cheered and embraced each other. Luke hugged his friends and assured Paul that he would keep vigilance over the city. "God established His church to bring glory to His Son, and we will not give up our work until the Son returns or God calls us to His side."

Lydia watched the joy and sadness mingle throughout the people before her. Though her heart welled up with pleasure at the new fellowship she shared with the believers, she felt a piece of her was missing. She had everything she could want, except Marcus.

THIRTEEN

After a night of too little sleep and too much emotion, the morning sun stung Lydia's eyes. She wrestled with the anxiety of what the day would bring. For her friends' safety, they had to leave the city. However, she felt more secure in her faith with them nearby. At least Luke would stay. He could help her when she felt weak, and perhaps with only one guest remaining, Marcus would come home.

The travelers ate a light breakfast and then finished packing their bags for the journey's next leg. They nodded in blessings over Lydia's home at each door frame and over each table.

"Are you sure that you want us to wait for you outside the city gates?" Lydia asked Paul. "We could stand with you in the forum when Takis makes his announcement and then follow you out to the place of prayer."

"It will be best if you wait with the others at the river," he answered. "Takis will make a public decree of our freedom, and then he will have his men escort us away. I do not want anyone else brought into a conflict needlessly. I do not expect a fight, but that may not be our choice. I believe Takis and his men will come to our defense, but the fewer to defend, the better. Your community will follow your lead, Lydia. Your calm example is more valuable to us today than any endorsing word."

Lydia conceded. She pulled her head covering up and secured it. Luke walked her to the front steps. "I will stand with them during the declaration and make sure that Calchas and Ercole do not make any claims against you or your household for housing us."

"That seems a little far-fetched, even for Calchas."

"You would be amazed at the far-fetched claims people make in resistance of the message of Jesus," Luke replied. "Sooner or later this thought, or a similar one, will occur to a man like Calchas."

"I am not worried about that," she said. "Calchas can claim whatever he wishes. Takis knows he ultimately answers to a higher voice. I only want your friends to know that we support them." She walked toward where the tree line began.

Luke nodded as he followed. "They know. And I will make sure that everyone who hears Takis' announcement about their departure knows that I will stay in the city as long as I can. It is important that you go to the river to pray, so others know that Calchas' attempts to persecute the believers in Philippi will not succeed."

Agatha joined them, saying to Lydia, "Joel and Phoebe will keep watch on the house while we are out."

Luke waved and left the women to continue their path to the river's edge. Lydia walked with Agatha through the busy marketplace, not giving a second glance to her closed shop. A few vendors hailed her, and she smiled and asked after their families. They knew she was on her way to pray, as usual, and wished her well.

Calchas stood in front of his booth with his arms crossed. He glared at Lydia and Agatha as they passed, scowling as though he had bettered them in a wrestling match and they had welched on their bets. A part of her was happy to know that she would not be in his sight when Takis announced that Paul and Silas were going free.

When they reached the river, the other believers greeted the women with kisses and blessings. Clement waited for everyone to find a place to sit and then began a prayer for his friends.

"Today our dear brothers leave our city. They brought us the message of truth, and now they will take this same word to others, near and far. Holy Father, we ask You to bless them in their travels. Bless the ears that will hear, and bless the hearts they will touch," he said. "Lord Jehovah, we ask for Your protection for Your servants as they are formally released from Takis' jurisdiction, and we ask that You bless our gathering and use us to increase Your kingdom."

As the time drew near for Paul, Silas, and Timothy to leave Philippi, tears flowed as freely as the river. Soon the small congregation moved from the water's edge to the road to meet the travelers.

Paul, Silas, Timothy and Luke marched through the city gates as boldly as when they arrived, but on this morning Takis' soldiers flanked them for a safe escort out of town. The group from the river surrounded them, and Luke offered a blessing, laying his hands on Paul, Silas and Timothy's shoulders, each in turn, as he prayed.

Silas began a psalm, and everyone joined him. Strangers on the road stopped to listen and stare at the odd gathering. Timothy smiled at them and invited them to be a part, but most went on through the city gates.

As the song ended, Paul held up his hand. "Dear friends, we are eager to take our message to Thessalonica. God is calling us there and beyond. I pray that you will not give up meeting with each other. Your love for each other will strengthen the message, as you all have strengthened me." He held out his hands to each person.

Gesturing to Lydia, he continued. "This sister has welcomed us as openly as she welcomed the Lord. She opened her home to the kingdom and to the church. Always show gratitude for her hospitality."

Silas nodded and looked up at the clouds in the sky. "We must be leaving you now, but remember us in your prayers."

Paul, Silas, and Timothy circled the group with warm embraces and kisses. Silas began singing as the three men started the next leg of their journey. The prayer group watched as the men disappeared down the road.

Luke thanked everyone for coming to see his partners off, and Lydia invited them to come to her home for evening prayers. "And bring others with you," she added. "There may be some in our town who were afraid to meet with us. Now that Paul and Silas have gone, they may be more open to listen."

Luke nodded. "Paul would be the first to agree. Invite everyone."

As the group dispersed, Luke gestured for Lydia to walk with him, and Agatha walked ahead and chatted with Euodia's maidservant.

"Was Takis embarrassed?" Lydia asked. "And was Calchas angry?"

Luke took a deep breath. "It is more than that. Takis handled his announcement with dignity—and the crowd was small at the time. When Calchas realized what was happening, though, he became furious."

"What did he do?" Lydia asked. "Will he try to hurt Paul and the others?"

Luke walked on, shaking his head and keeping his voice low. "I do not think so." He slowed his pace slightly. "He yelled. He called Takis a few profane names. I do not believe he will be in a position to ask for any favors for a while. Takis warned him that any attempt to interfere with Paul's travels will be dealt with harshly." Luke sighed. "I think your magistrate is feeling lots of pressure right now."

Lydia grimaced. She was relieved not to have witnessed such a sight. "You still sound somber. What else happened?" She stopped in the road and held Luke's arm.

"I cannot say for sure, but Calchas closed his booth in a hurry. He was muttering something. I did not understand much of what he said, but I heard your name, and your cousin's."

Lydia held her hands over her heart. "I cannot imagine

Calchas would do anything to hurt Marcus," she said with a tremor in her voice. "But I never imagined he could be so brutal against Paul and Silas, or against Daphne, either."

Luke held up his hands. "I did not hear any threats."

Lydia did not wait to hear more. "Agatha, go on home. Luke and I are going to see Marcus."

"Yes, Mistress." Agatha turned toward the house, accompanied by Euodia's maidservant.

Lydia quickened her pace, leading Luke toward Calchas' house. As they approached, they saw Ercole and Marcus on either side of a donkey. Just seeing Marcus put Lydia at ease. She hurried to his side.

"Marcus, are you all right?" She put her hands on his shoulders. Luke stayed back a few steps to give her room to talk.

Marcus pulled free of her reach. "What do you want, Lydia?" He barely looked up as he fastened a blanket and a leather pack to the donkey's saddle.

She took a deep breath. "I want you to come home, Marcus. I love you. I want to know that you are all right. I am concerned."

"There is no reason for you to worry," he said as if he spoke to a customer in the forum. "I am grown now. I do not need anyone looking after me."

"Please..." She started to reach for him again, but he shifted farther away.

"I will not go back to your house."

Lydia sighed. "At least let me help you," she said in a quiet tone. She did not want to embarrass her cousin in front of Ercole.

"Marcus does not need anyone's help," Calchas boomed from behind her.

Luke turned to see his heavy-set figure approaching.

Lydia clutched her hands together, hoping that no one else could see them tremble. She wished she had the chance to reason with Marcus alone. "Calchas, he is my family."

"You have already shown him how you treat your family, Lydia. He is the least of your concerns now—as you have established." Calchas clicked his tongue as he came around the side of the donkey to stand next to Marcus. "He has chosen his friends as you have chosen yours."

Lydia searched Marcus's face for answers. "What have I done to hurt you?"

"What have you done?" Marcus scoffed. "You chose others over me. You ridicule my beliefs. You treat me like a child."

Lydia felt crushed. She shook her head. "Oh, Marcus, I never intended to..."

"I need to get on the road. Do you have anything else to say?" Marcus took a small leather pouch from Calchas and tucked it into a fold in his sash.

Helpless to do more, Lydia went around the burdened donkey to her cousin's side. "Where are you going?"

Marcus walked away from her to pick up a bedroll for his trip. "Calchas is sending me to Delphi."

"What?" she asked. "Delphi is too far away."

"And I am just a child?" Marcus spat back.

"I did not say that," Lydia insisted.

"Yes, you did."

She chewed on her lip and took a deep breath to start over. "I am sorry. Please believe me. I am."

Marcus looked at Calchas and Ercole as if they had answers for him. They just shrugged. He glanced at Luke and then back to Lydia, frowning. "It is too late. I must go."

Lydia shook her head again. "Do not leave, Marcus. Not yet."

"I can go where I like," he said in a firm tone.

"I just want to talk to you."

"Perhaps when I return." He looked over the donkey and his equipment. "I have business to conduct. Your friends took Daphne from Calchas."

"They helped her. She was sick, and they healed her," she said.

"And then you bought her," he whispered. "This is why I am going to Delphi. Philippi needs a fortune-teller, and I am returning with one!"

Calchas chuckled as Lydia coughed in dismay. He grinned through a sneer. "You will be happy to know that your generous payment will provide our city with another oracle. At a profit. A handsome profit."

Lydia pulled her attention away from Calchas and his toxic assertions. She would gain nothing meeting Calchas in a dispute over whether Philippi did or did not need an intoxicated virgin to tell it what its future held. She breathed in and out several times and then turned her attention to the only one present who really mattered to her at that moment. "I just want you back home." She reached for Marcus. "I want to restore what has been lost."

Marcus shook his head in disgust and took another step

away. He glared at Luke. "Take care of her." He took the reins in hand and coaxed the donkey to its feet. Smiling at Ercole and Calchas, he said, "I will return soon, and then you will be the proud owners of the best oracle outside of Delphi."

Calchas nodded. "Do not tarry long. Every day without a seer is a silver piece lost."

Ercole waved. "Take care, Marcus."

Without turning around again, Marcus led the donkey away toward the west gate. Calchas turned to Ercole and said, "Go back to the forum, Ercole. You must tend the shop alone. Today has been trying, and I must rest." As Ercole departed, Calchas turned and retreated into the darkness of his home.

Luke took Lydia's arm and gestured toward her house. "Let us go. Perhaps rest will be good for us all."

She nodded and leaned on Luke's arm as they walked. Lydia's mind raced with one worry after another. She imagined all manner of dangers on the road—stormy weather, ruffians, impassable crossings and novel temptations from far off places. "Marcus is not experienced," she whispered, more to herself than to Luke.

"And you will pray for his safety," he said.

"I feel as though I should be doing more," she sobbed.

"What is more powerful than calling on the creator of the universe?"

She gazed into his dark eyes and blinked at his simple reasoning. "I just let him leave."

Luke nodded. "Yes, but first you told him that you loved him. Whatever he says about his friends, they do not offer him love. He knows that he can find that with you."

Lydia shrugged. "Will God protect him? Marcus does not want to have anything to do with God."

"God is patient with all of us, even those who resist Him." Luke smiled. "I have seen harder hearts than Marcus's turn to God."

Lydia prayed as she walked.

Ercole ran up from behind and hailed them. "Wait, Lydia. May I speak with you for a moment?"

Lydia and Luke turned to face the young man. The three of them stood at the split in the road. Ercole would soon take the path to the left, heading back to the shops, and Lydia and Luke would go right, toward home.

"What is it that you require of me, Ercole?" Lydia asked, already exhausted.

"You said that Daphne was sick and that your friends healed her?" he asked.

"Yes, I did. Yes, they did. You saw."

Ercole looked at Luke as if he was studying the man. "You are a doctor?"

Lydia saw a hint of a smile form on Luke's lips. "I am, but I did nothing to heal her. Paul called on the great Physician to heal her."

"The great... I do not understand." Ercole glanced at Lydia and back to Luke. "What do you mean?"

"He called out, in the name of Jesus, the demons of poison that held Daphne captive to her visions." Luke looked in Ercole's glassy eyes. "You have seen the visions, too?"

Ercole nodded.

"They frighten you?"

"Yes."

A breeze blew past them, and goose bumps rose on Ercole's arms, contrasting with the sweat on his brow. Lydia tilted her head, trying to understand.

"Do the demons haunt you, Ercole?" she asked.

He shook his head. "Your friend took her visions away with just a word."

Luke took a breath. "Paul did nothing of his own power. Jesus Christ worked through him. God healed the girl."

"And we called on our gods to restore her visions. We did everything we could think to do. We sacrificed. We offered incense. We chanted. We prayed."

"To what god?" Luke asked.

"We prayed to Apollo first, and then Zeus when Apollo did not answer." Ercole rubbed his arms to warm them.

"Perhaps they are not so powerful," Luke suggested, knowing he was taking a risk.

Lydia watched Ercole's expression as he listened to Luke. He did not seem to get angry—just confused.

"Zeus is the highest god, and Apollo is the god of the oracle. They have more power..." Ercole's words faded. "But they could not give her back the sight."

Luke nodded. "No, they could not. Our God is king of the world. He created everything that has been created. He can heal, and He can destroy."

"But you can call on your god. You can control him?" Ercole asked.

Luke laughed. "If any man controls a god, he is not much of a god, is he?"

Ercole looked as though the thought never occurred to him. "I have to go to my shop." He put his hand on Lydia's shoulder. "Do not worry for Marcus. Calchas gave him everything he will need for the journey, and Marcus is a bright boy."

Lydia considered his point and nodded. "Thank you, Ercole."

Ercole dipped his chin and turned to hurry to his booth. Lydia watched him for a moment, and then asked, "What was that?"

Luke allowed some of his optimism to infuse his expression. "I believe your friend is curious about Jesus. We must pray for his heart to be softened."

Lydia sighed. "I will." She walked on. The sunlight filtered through the trees and flickered on her face as she strolled through the grove. Luke remained quiet until they approached the edge of the clearing.

"Jesus would often pray in a garden filled with olive trees," he said. "I know why, now. The leaves are beautiful. It is peaceful. The breeze is like the very breath of God."

Lydia blinked in astonishment. "My husband, Simeon, used to say the same thing—the breath of God." Her heart pounded and swelled. "Just when I need to hear his voice."

Luke laughed. "God knows your every need."

Lydia faced her home. She wanted to spend hours talking with Luke. She missed the times she used to linger in the trees with Simeon and talk about the day. She missed feeling important enough to a man to have him confide in her, as a friend and an equal and an intelligent being in her own right. The more she considered staying with Luke, the more she felt that she should not. "I think I need some time alone before the house fills with people tonight."

Luke nodded, with a hint of regret, and gestured to the house. "If you wish to go inside then I will stay here for a while."

"To pray?" she asked.

"Yes. Though the sky looks calm now, I feel that a storm is coming."

CHAPTER

FOURTEEN

"More pain," Daphne said. "The other girls like me are filled with the same demons. We cannot sleep without monsters and other horrors. And waking is almost as bad."

"But what you saw—it was not real," Korinna said. "Ghosts and spirits did not really speak to you. Did they?"

Daphne shrugged. "I cannot say what was spirit and what was demon. It all felt real. I saw visions of people without arms or faces. I saw blood all the time. I had dreams of friends being eaten by lions or vultures." She shivered. "I often thought I was falling up into the sky."

Korinna gasped and looked at Lydia. "You have saved us both." She reached for Lydia's hand.

"I have done nothing." Lydia squeezed both girls' hands. "God has brought you both into my household, and for that I give thanks."

Korinna held up the piece of fabric on which she worked.

She sewed a dark purple thread into a leaf pattern around the edge. "Is this what you wanted?" she asked.

Lydia nodded. "This is exquisite, dear. I feel a pang of guilt for even acknowledging your creation since you made this work of art on the Sabbath, a day of rest, but I cannot bring myself to hide it just because you could not wait another day to give it to the world." She held the needlework out to allow Agatha to see.

Korinna raised her brows and laughed. "Embroidering is so much easier than cleaning floors that I forget it is still work. But I will put this away until morning."

Daphne took the fabric from her to keep Korinna from having to get up and down. "Allow me to put it up for you, please."

Korinna smiled in appreciation. "Thank you, child. That is very considerate of you."

Agatha and Lydia exchanged smiles. "Korinna, how old are you?" Lydia asked.

"I will be seventeen next month." She leaned back, and her growing belly became more pronounced.

Agatha turned to the younger child. "What about you, Daphne? How old are you?"

Daphne looked down at her feet. "I am thirteen years old."

Lydia nodded. "When I was sixteen I married Simeon. Agatha was given to me as my maidservant a week before our wedding."

Agatha added, "You were never cruel to me even once, even as many others are cruel to their slaves all the time. You have cared for me as much as I have cared for you, and you provided a safe and comfortable home for me. You offered me my freedom so many times I have lost count."

Daphne and Korinna turned to the older women with shocked expressions. "You are free?" Daphne asked.

"I am as free as I choose to be," Agatha answered. "I have a friend in Lydia unlike any other. She has nursed me when I was sick. She offered her shoulder when I had a broken heart. And I am more than proud to say that I have had opportunities to do the same for her."

Korinna and Daphne smiled as they listened to Agatha.

Lydia nodded. "We love each other. Our fates, our destinies are joined. I will never separate us."

Korinna grimaced and looked at her hands. Her smile distorted, and she blinked back tears. "I said the same for my dear husband, Judah."

"As I did about my Simeon," Lydia added. "And Agatha is still by my side." Lydia thought for a moment. "Truth be known, so is Simeon."

Korinna took a deep breath, and Daphne smiled up at her, patting her knee. "You are strong, Korinna. God will help you just as He has helped me." She looked at Lydia. "And I am here to help you in any way I can."

Agatha smiled at Lydia, who again took both girls' hands in her own. "Nothing would make me happier than if you two would become the same kind of friends as we are. In this world, we all need someone who will stay with us to the end. That kind of devotion only comes from those to whom we, ourselves, are devoted."

All four women became quiet, each contemplating the lesson Lydia had imparted to them. In time Lydia gathered herself, stood and said, "It is time to begin preparing for tonight's meeting. So much has happened since our first fellowship that we do not know how many people to expect. We must be ready for anything."

Luke came into the great hall and greeted the women. "Lydia, there is a young man here to speak with you."

Lydia saw a youth standing in the door and gestured for him to enter. When he did, she could see that it was Marcus' friend, Epaphroditus.

"Good day, Epaphroditus. You are here early," she said with a warm smile.

Epaphroditus offered a small bow to Lydia and the other women. "Good day. I have come to see if I may help prepare for this evening's gathering. I thought that, since the other men left, you might need another hand."

Luke smiled and nodded in appreciation and in welcome. "We would be happy to have you." He gestured to the court-yard. "Let us clear the yard while the women see to the household needs. Tonight, we will celebrate the Lord's Supper."

Epaphroditus nodded. Before he followed Luke, he paused at Lydia's side. "I have been praying for Marcus to join us soon."

Lydia nodded. "Thank you. So have I."

Epaphroditus took her hand. "He and I had been wrestling together at the palaestra for many months. He has missed our matches for the last few days, though. Is he ill?"

Lydia shrugged. "He has a sickness in his heart, I think. But the reason he has not met you at the palaestra is that he is traveling to Delphi for Calchas. Please continue to lift him up to the Lord. He needs our prayers more than ever."

Epaphroditus nodded. "I will pray for Marcus," he said. "And for you."

The men went to work preparing the yard for guests, and the women began making some food. Soon the house filled with the smells of bread and spices and the sounds of friends greeting each other. Lydia and Luke stood at the open front door welcoming guests. Luke looked up to the darkening sky and frowned.

"I think we might be moving the meeting inside," he said.

Lydia nodded as a gust of wind caught the door and pushed it back against her wall. "I will tell Joel. I am sure that we will have plenty of room. The crowd is smaller tonight."

Lydia went looking for Joel. Along the way, she found Phoebe, who was standing next to Agatha peering out toward the yard. Both women wore the broad smiles of collaborators, smiles that widened the longer they stared out.

"What is it?" Lydia asked.

Agatha and Phoebe jumped at her voice. Agatha pulled Lydia to stand between her and Phoebe and pointed out to where Epaphroditus was sitting—on a bench next to Daphne. "Look at them," she whispered.

Lydia smiled with sudden insight. "Now please do not make trouble for them by spreading rumors. They are both young. Daphne needs friends; she has never had one before. Let them be friends."

Agatha and Phoebe giggled. "You are right, Mistress," they said without conviction.

Lydia turned them to face her. "I mean it. Do not cause them suffer to for sins you make up for them. Leave them to the night. Now. Phoebe, you tell Joel and all the others that we need to move inside for tonight's worship. The weather is turning harsh. Agatha, you see to moving the tables and utensils into the great room. Hurry, now. I smell rain."

Both women nodded, and within a few minutes, the small crowd gathered in the great hall. Arsene and his family were the last to arrive, and as his wife and son found their seats, Arsene found a place at Luke's side.

"May I sing the song that Paul and Silas were singing in the jail?" he asked.

Luke nodded with a sincere smile. "I think that would be appropriate tonight."

Arsene took a few steps into the room, and the congregation grew quiet. Arsene's muscular frame towered over most of the people present. As a Roman conscript, he commanded respect. As a man, his very presence demanded attention. He held out his hands, as though he were pleading with them. Every eye in the room focused on him.

"I want to share with all of you the song that saved my life. I heard it for the first time two nights ago, when I was only a jailer, and Paul and Silas were only criminals against Rome's law. Despite their confinement, despite Rome's threats against them and everyone they loved, in spite of the hopelessness of their peril, they sang. Then there was the earthquake. And now all of us are free." Arsene took a deep breath and began singing. His rich tones rolled over the group and filled the whole house. As he formed the words, his eyes filled with tears that rushed in rivers down his craggy face. His entire body moved with the song, and as he finished the house fell silent and still and filled with quiet tears.

The front door burst open. A rush of wind whipped through the room, lifting, swirling, and lapping at hair and clothing. As quickly as the hammer blow of wind began, it disappeared again when Joel pushed the door closed and secured the latch. Everyone in the room scurried to recover blowing baskets and table coverings, wondering at how strong and sudden the storm came upon them and concerned about how much worse it would get.

When everyone had resumed his seat, Arsene addressed them. "I do not know about you, but I no longer fear the storm. A storm is just another of God's creations, and every storm contains the blessing of fresher air and softer light when it finally clears. Let us be at peace, my friends, and celebrate the One who brings both storms and calm." Arsene began singing the song again, and this time everyone else joined him. The music echoed from the walls and ceiling, ringing through the tiled roof and out into the night.

At the last word of the song—at the very last syllable—it seemed to Lydia that God pronounced "Amen" with a clap of thunder that shook the floor beneath them.

Chills ran up her back, and when she looked at Luke's reaction, he only smiled, and she could see that he, too, was affected by the thunderous ovation to God's hymn. She knew that he had seen even more magnificent displays than this, but it was clear that he was no more afraid than Arsene.

When Arsene finished singing, Luke stood up to address the group.

"My friends, you are here tonight because of your faith in the God of creation. The Lord of the storm is the Lord of still waters and peaceful skies as well. Our Father teaches us to love one another, to show kindness, and reach out in peace to our neighbors." He regarded Lydia. "As our sister has done, providing us with a safe place of fellowship." Luke continued. "Our faith does not threaten; that was not Jesus' way. Our faith is a message of peace and joy."

His expression turned serious. "But the time is coming," Luke said. "Indeed, it is already here. We will be ridiculed. We will be flogged. We will be executed for our faith in God."

Many in the group began to whisper to each other and nod. "Takis will take care for a while, but it will not last," Luke continued. "What happened to Paul and Silas will serve to spread the news of Jesus. They left Philippi to take the message westward. Others who saw what happened will travel in every direction. They will tell the story of a girl held captive by demons, who was healed—calmed at the mention of the name of Jesus Christ."

The group cheered and gestured to Daphne. She thanked those around her.

Luke gestured to Arsene. "This man will tell everyone he knows about the night he almost took his own life for fear of Roman retribution."

Arsene pounded his fist across his chest. "I now serve a higher kingdom."

"Amen," several shouted.

Luke reached out to the crowd. "Church, we must be

strong in our faith. We must be generous with our blessings and reach out in God's love to everyone around us. When others see you, make sure that you show them that Christ lives in you. People will know that you are following Jesus because of the way you show love to others."

"How do we show love to those who want to hurt us?" Alexander asked. He held his wife close at his side.

Luke nodded. "We show love to those who want to hurt us by refraining from responding to their hostility with our own." He looked up from Alexander to address the rest of the gathering. "That is the challenge we face every day. Jesus did not tell us to treat others with love only until they treated us with violence. Jesus told us to treat everyone with love, even those who would harm us. As he did. Jesus did not stay only in safe places. Jesus did not spend His days in palaces or even in homes as lovely as this. He touched the lepers, the blind and lame, the young and old, the tax collectors and the harlots. Jesus spoke to the rich and the deprived. He held nothing back. Even after His enemies nailed Him to a cross, He forgave them."

"We can forgive. We can pray," Epaphroditus said. "We can befriend the friendless." He glanced down to Daphne and smiled. "We can speak kindness to those who ridicule us."

Luke nodded. "This young man is right. And when he is feeling weak and alone in his faith…?" As Luke's voice faded, the sound of heavy rain filled the air.

Daphne listened for a moment and then stood at Epaphroditus' side. "He will not be alone," she said.

One by one, each person in the room joined her and

stood up. When everyone was standing, Alexander started a song. The church sang one song and then another until Luke knelt and began to pray.

He prayed for Paul, Silas, and Timothy, and for all whom they would touch with God's message. He prayed for Takis and for Rome. He prayed for Marcus.

Before leaving the house, the crowd all celebrated Jesus' resurrection with communion. As they finished their worship, Lydia asked Luke to invite the group to stay if they wished. She did not want to send anyone out into the storm.

As the night progressed, the squall lightened. Lydia and Luke moved out to the front portico as people began to venture out. When the last guest left, Lydia looked up to the sky, hoping to see a few stars.

"I think it is still too clouded for stars," Luke said. "Do not worry, Lydia," he continued, somehow knowing exactly what was in her mind. "Marcus is a smart young man. He will surely find shelter for the night."

"It is not only the weather that concerns me," she said. "Traveling alone is dangerous, and Marcus is relying on charms and amulets for protection."

"But you are praying for him," Luke assured her. "We all are."

She nodded. "Will God protect those who reject him so vehemently?"

Luke took her hand. It felt strong—warm and gentle over her own. "God loves Marcus," he reminded her. "Jesus did not only face death for those who love Him. He died for all people. And Lydia, God loves you. He does not want to see you worried. He wants you to trust Him."

Lydia took a deep breath, filled with the cleansing smell of rain. "Forgive me, Lord, for my doubt," she whispered. "Protect my cousin and return him to me." She paused for a second, and another thought took hold of her mind. "Lord God, I am selfish. I apologize for my selfishness. Lord, You are the King, and Your will is always right. Help Marcus to see that and know that. Help him to come to You, whatever it takes for that."

Luke smiled at her and squeezed her hand. "You are brave in your prayers."

Lydia nodded and looked up into Luke's eyes. "That is what scares me," she answered. "I know that I am praying for a miracle."

CHAPTER

FIFTEEN

The days passed, and Lydia continued the same prayer. "Lord, bring Marcus back to us safely and turn his heart to You, by whatever means You will." The church meetings in her home again grew in attendance. Luke spent time each day in the marketplace and at the theater speaking to anyone who would listen. Several travelers spent the evening with the group, singing and praying and eating. Luke did most of the speaking, but Arsene shared his own story night after night, inspiring the residents of Philippi to become bolder in their faith.

"You know," Lydia said one morning after Luke had baptized several more believers. "If our meetings continue to increase like this, you will have this whole town believing in Jesus."

Luke eyed Calchas, who was walking around the courtyard and drumming up business for his idols and charms.

"That is my goal," he replied. "And God is doing a mighty work here, despite the challenges."

Lydia nodded and tipped her chin to Ercole. He stood at the front of his booth and welcomed his customers. "Your business is lively today," she said with a smile.

Ercole grinned. "Yes, and your shop is doing well."

Lydia agreed. "The Lord blesses me, and I am grateful." She paused for a second, wondering if she should continue. For a few days, she felt an urge to invite him to her home, but she was afraid of what Calchas might do. As she thought about asking again, the words formed on her lips, almost on their own. "Would you join us for supper this evening, Ercole?"

He blinked with surprise. "You would have me to your house for a meal?"

She nodded. "Of course, we are friends, Ercole. I would be honored for you to come."

The young man stared at her for a second as if he was confused. Before he could answer, a customer approached him, asking about some silver charms. He nodded to Lydia and then went inside his booth.

"Bold," was all Luke whispered to Lydia as she walked past him to see to a customer of her own.

Lydia smiled and whispered back, "Faith."

She helped an older woman select an appropriate cut of fabric for a head covering and a spool of thread to match. The woman was almost ready to leave when she saw a piece of embroidery on a scarf. She picked up the scarf and held it in the sunlight to examine it more carefully.

"I must have this, too," the woman told Lydia. "This

color thread is breath-taking." She fingered the needlework. "Did you do this?"

Lydia shook her head. "No, but a young woman who lives in my home did. Her name is Korinna, and she does beautiful work."

The woman sighed. "When I was a young girl I did this kind of embroidery." She stretched out her hand so that Lydia could see how her knuckles and fingers were bent and twisted with age and arthritis. "I did such lovely work that I was commissioned to sew for the palace in Rome. This thread color was reserved only for Caesar in those days."

Lydia remembered her father telling her about the dark reddish purple being the color of kings. As the Roman Empire spread and brought peace and prosperity, more people could afford the luxuries of purple dyes and fabrics.

"You must have been blessed with incredible talent," Lydia said with a smile.

The older woman beamed. "This scarf will remind me of the household in which I once served."

Lydia helped her complete her purchase and wished her well as she left the shop. Even as the woman walked away, Lydia's heart dwelled on her words. *The household in which I serve.*

Luke smiled as if he could see the gears of her mind turning. "What are you thinking?" he asked. He watched as her eyes scanned the booth.

Lydia strode to the back of the shop and picked up a spool of dark crimson cording. "Would this work?" she asked him.

Luke glanced at the cord and looked back at Lydia's expression. "Work for what?"

"We could use this. Perhaps we could give everyone a piece, as a reminder of whose house it is that we serve." She nodded as the idea developed. "This little cut of purple can remind us of our faith in God's promise of salvation."

Luke thought about this, the question appearing on his face before he gave it voice. "Do you think our church needs something physical to remind them? We do not want them to prize a possession over their faith."

Lydia shook her head. "The cloth is not a substitute for faith but rather a symbol of it. It is not something to worship but something to remind us of our commitment—to God and to each other. If it were a substitute for faith, then Calchas would insist on selling it, himself. Let us treat this as a gift that will serve as a reminder. Nothing more."

Luke nodded. "Tonight, we will give each believer a piece, and I will tell them about this woman, and what she said to you." He looked at Lydia and sighed. "Your generosity is a blessing, you know. For each person to have some of this cording will cost you the entire spool. Are you certain that you want to sacrifice that much?"

Lydia patted his shoulder. "I would be honored to offer it. I have been blessed by the Lord with all of this," she gestured to all of her merchandise, "and I choose to use it to bless the Lord in return."

Luke motioned to the front of the booth, and Lydia turned to see Ercole waiting for her.

"Yes, my friend," she said, approaching him with a broad smile. "Have you decided to join us for supper tonight?"

Ercole glanced over his shoulder toward Calchas, and Lydia detected a trace of fear in his expression. "I do not think I should eat with you tonight, but perhaps another time." Ercole cleared his throat and lowered his voice. "Calchas is upset. He expected Marcus to return this morning with our new seer. Without word from him, Calchas is growing anxious."

Lydia held her breath. "Marcus was to return today? It has only been ten days since he left. Perhaps the weather has delayed him. He is cautious, you know."

Ercole nodded, with a look of hope in his eyes. "That is what I told Calchas. I do not wish to worry you, but I thought you should know. I am sure that Marcus is well, and he will probably return tomorrow. I just thought your church might pray for him."

Luke listened and reached out to grasp Ercole's wrist in thanks. "You are a good friend to Marcus and Lydia. We will pray for Marcus and for the girl traveling with him. It would bless our gathering if you came, too. Your presence would be a great comfort for Lydia."

Lydia's hands covered her heart, and she was already praying for her cousin. Ercole stared at her and then looked back to Luke. "I do not know... perhaps..."

"Ercole!" Calchas shouted from within his booth. "Come! At once!"

"Perhaps," Ercole repeated and excused himself.

Before Lydia could say a word, Luke took her elbow and led her to the bench along the wall of the shop. "Sit down. Rest. Seek peace for yourself."

Lydia sat down and finished her prayer. When she

finished, she joined Luke at the front of the booth.

"I can watch for your customers until Agatha comes," he said. "Take the time you need."

Lydia grimaced and sniffed. "God asked me to believe in Him, and ever since I was a young woman, I have believed in Him. Jesus asked me to trust in Him, and I have taken a vow to do so." She sighed and settled her hands on her hips. "Faith and trust mean nothing if they are only words. If every time a trouble crosses my path I fret and carry on about it, I deny my faith. You have taught me this. If I really trust the Lord to take care of Marcus, I will listen and obey."

Luke sighed and shook his head. "You remind me of Timothy's mother, Eunice. She listens to the Lord's voice and speaks His direction in her life."

"If I do not speak it, I fear I will not live up to it," Lydia said. "You can hold me accountable."

Luke laughed. "That is what church is all about, I think."

Later as they waited at the door for friends to arrive, Luke told Lydia about the women who followed Jesus with the apostles. "They worked very hard to support His ministry. Some of them sold the garments they had sewn, and some sold food they had prepared. Some of the women made blankets and pottery. One woman made perfumes. They all used their gifts to provide for Jesus and his apostles. Some women gave up everything they had to follow Him alongside the men."

Lydia shook her head. "What a difficult life that would be," she said.

Luke laughed at her response. "Some might say the same

about a woman who opens her home every night to a house full of people, expecting nothing in return."

Alexander and Theda were the first to arrive for the evening worship, and Luke handed them each a few inches of cording. "Hold on to these," he instructed them. "We will talk about them in a little while."

Theda and Alexander took the cords and went inside to see Phoebe. As each family arrived, they took their pieces of cord and joined the others. When the courtyard was half-full, Luke left Lydia at the door to greet her guests, and he went in to see that everyone was seated and comfortable.

Lydia could hear Arsene singing, and she felt a swelling in her heart. She listened as Clement led a prayer of thanksgiving for the young church. He prayed for Paul, Silas and Timothy, and for all who heard their message. She could hear him praying for Marcus, too. She closed her eyes tightly and asked the Lord to protect her cousin.

She intended to close the door and join the group, but when she opened her eyes again, she saw Ercole running toward her house. She reached out to him as he hurried up her steps.

"Do you have word of Marcus?" she asked, seeing the urgency in his face.

"Yes, Lydia, but it is not good." Ercole took her hands and pulled her to the bench by her door.

She sat down beside her friend and stared at him, willing him to speak. Her trembling lips could not form any words, and her mind froze. Suddenly a breeze swept through the portico, and Lydia could smell a faint fragrance of flowers. A sense of calm settled over her, and she could breathe again.

"What has happened?" she asked.

Ercole took a deep breath. "Marcus is back, and he is alive, but he was badly beaten. He told Calchas that robbers had attacked him on the road as he was returning to Philippi. He came back with nothing. He said the thieves took the girl, the donkey, and all of the money."

"Where is he?" she asked. "I will bring him home and take care of him. Luke is a doctor. If Marcus is injured, he can help."

Ercole shook his head. "It is worse than that, Lydia. Calchas does not believe him. He accuses him of stealing the money and pretending to be hurt and robbed."

"Oh, no!" she gasped. "Marcus would not lie."

Ercole nodded. "I told Calchas that, but he is furious. He has taken formal charges to Takis. Can you come and speak for Marcus?"

Lydia quickly took the basket of cording inside and called for Joel.

"Yes, Mistress," he answered.

"I need to go back to the forum with Ercole. Marcus has returned, and he is in trouble." Lydia secured her epiblema over her hair. "Tell the others to pray for him."

"Yes, Mistress," Joel replied and rejoined the group.

Lydia and Ercole hurried back to the agora, arriving to see Takis pacing in front of her cousin. Marcus looked like a child kneeling before the magistrate. A small crowd circled the assembly.

Lydia could see large bruises and abrasions on Marcus's arms and legs. His hair looked matted, and his face was red with cuts and scratches. She could not hold back the tears for her cousin.

"Do you have an answer to Calchas' charge?" Takis asked. He held his chin high, not daring to look Marcus in the face.

Marcus sniffed and sobbed. He cast a sideways glance at Calchas and shook his head. "I did not steal his money. I was attacked by robbers."

Lydia could see that Marcus's eyes were swollen with dark circles around them.

Calchas scoffed. Some of the people watching spat on Marcus and jeered at his answer, too.

"And do you not have anyone to speak on your behalf?" Takis asked.

Calchas glared at Ercole when he realized that his own partner had brought Lydia to Marcus's side.

Lydia stepped forward. "I will speak for my cousin," she said as loudly as she could manage. "He is a good man. He is honest and trustworthy. If he were not, then Calchas never would have sent him on this task in the first place."

Takis turned to face Calchas and raised his brows.

Calchas rolled his eyes. "I was kind and generous to him, and he took advantage of me!" he shouted with indignation.

"He admires you," Lydia responded. "He wants nothing more than your approval. He would do nothing to jeopardize that."

Takis blinked casually as he oversaw the hearing. He looked at Lydia and sighed. "Do you have anything more to add to his defense?"

"Just a question," Lydia replied. "Where are they?"

"Where are what?" Takis asked.

"The money. The girl. The donkey. Has anyone searched Marcus's home or other places he frequents to see if the missing items are there? If they cannot be found, then how can anyone be so sure that Marcus is lying about being robbed?"

Calchas issued an explosive snort. "Rubbish. He could have a thousand confederates along the road willing to take my money and property and put them where they can never be found. You prove nothing."

Lydia swallowed hard and looked at Ercole, begging him to speak up for her cousin. When he remained silent, she added, "I have raised Marcus in my home from the time he was a small child. I know his heart. He is eager to become a respected citizen of Philippi. He would not lie or steal from anyone. I believe in him."

"Why do we listen to this woman?" Calchas whined. "She was once esteemed in our city. But now she socializes with troublemakers. She stirs up discord among our citizens. She befriended the travelers who caused the near-destruction of my business." Calchas shot a harsh glare toward Takis. "Her friends have already caused problems for you, Takis. Do not forget that, brother."

Takis sniffed and chewed on his lip. He paced back to stand directly in front of Marcus. "Marcus, you leave me little choice. You have only your relative to speak for you—a relative who has been the source of much grief for me and for other prominent citizens of late. You have no witness to say that you did not do these things of which you are accused."

Lydia dropped to her knees at Marcus's side. "Takis,

please," she begged. "Can you not see how he has suffered? He needs someone to tend to his wounds. He is hurt."

Takis turned his gaze back to Calchas and nodded. "The evidence is clear to me. Marcus left Philippi with Calchas' money. He has returned without it. Calchas, what will you require?"

Lydia listened and prayed in her heart. She could not believe the cruelty of these men.

Calchas cleared his throat and inflated his chest. "I request that Marcus receives a fair punishment. He should be flogged as a liar and a thief and should be jailed until he can repay the money he took from me, as well as compensation for my donkey and my new seer."

It took Lydia several seconds to process what Calchas had said. "What?" she said through a rush of tears. "Your request is unreasonable. He is not a common criminal! I will pay whatever you ask, Calchas. Do not have him lashed and jailed as well. I beg your mercy."

Takis looked at Calchas for his reply to her plea.

"I am afraid I have no mercy for *your* cousin, Lydia," he said. He looked at Takis and pointed at Marcus. "I demand justice here."

Takis snapped his fingers and, just as with Paul and Silas, two of his guards pulled Marcus's already-ripped tunic away to bare his back. A third soldier brought out a leather strap and marched to the young man's side.

Lydia wept and reached out for her cousin. "NO!" she screamed. "Do not touch him!"

Ercole pulled her away from the scene as the soldier began striking Marcus with the whip. Through the dense curtain of watchers, Lydia could see blood and hear Marcus shrieking in pain.

Lydia struggled to free herself from Ercole's grip, but she was already weak from crying. The more she fought against his arms, the weaker she became. The beating seemed to last for hours, though Lydia knew it was only a few minutes. She could hear bystanders calling Marcus every sort of derogatory name. All she could do was weep.

At the end of the flogging, the two soldiers took Marcus away to the jail. Takis raised his nose above the crowd and declared, "Calchas will bring me an appropriate settlement that shall be paid before Marcus will be released. He will report this amount to me within the week, and I will level any additional fines at that time." Takis stared down his nose at Lydia. "The matter is settled."

Lydia crumbled into a heap on the ground as the crowd scattered and Takis returned to his office. Ercole sat for a moment by her side. "Perhaps I can talk to Calchas," he muttered.

"Why would you not speak for Marcus? A word from you..."

"Would not have made any difference," Ercole replied. "It would have only added to Calchas' fury. I am not strong like you, Lydia."

"Ercole!" Calchas shouted from across the forum. "Come away from her. Now!"

Ercole grimaced and left Lydia alone in the dust. She watched as every other person left the square and went home for the night. The last golden ray of sunlight slipped away behind the mountain ridge, and the whole town turned a rich purple.

"Lord God, King of the universe," Lydia whispered. "Hear my plea for mercy. You are sovereign and holy above all earthly things. Your wisdom outweighs the heights of man's dreams and imagination. Lord, I ask that You protect my dear Marcus and draw him to You." She felt the ache in her side fade. She thought she could hear voices calling her name, but she could see no one. "Lord, show me how to reach him with Your love."

She looked all around her for the source of the voices but saw nothing. The purple sky grew thick and black.

CHAPTER

SIXTEEN

"Are you all right?" Agatha whispered as Lydia tried to open her eyes.

The sunlight flooding through her bedroom window made it difficult for Lydia to focus on anything. Slowly Agatha's figure formed beside her.

"What happened?" she asked.

Agatha looked at Lydia with concern and compassion. "You fainted last night in the forum. We tried to revive you but could not, so we carried you home. I was afraid..."

"I think I remember." She started to sit upright in her bed, but as she raised her head, a sharp pain lanced through her temples. She closed her eyes tightly and held her breath.

"Just rest now," Agatha warned her. "I will tell Luke you are awake. Perhaps he can bring you something for the pain."

The memories of what happened to Marcus came back to Lydia in a rush. "Is Marcus still in prison?"

Agatha nodded. "Yes. Joel went to speak to Takis this

morning and was told that Marcus is still in custody. He tried to find out what the fines will be, but Takis will not tell him."

"I must go," Lydia said, trying again to sit up. She felt as if the room were turning around her. Her stomach tightened in a knot, and a clammy sweat covered her skin. As she tried to speak, her lips began to tremble. She pressed them together tightly to fight her nausea.

Agatha shook her head and eased her back against the cushions. "I think it is unwise for you to go anywhere just now, Lydia. Please be patient."

After a few minutes, Luke brought her a small bowl of clear broth. "Sip this slowly," he instructed. "It will help your head."

Lydia drank the warm liquid in short sips until it was gone. It tasted bitter and salty. As it soothed her throat, she realized how much her whole body ached.

"When can I get up and take care of my cousin?" she asked. Her voice sounded scratchy in her own ears.

Luke almost laughed. "Lydia, you remind me of a donkey with four broken legs who insists on trying to walk. You must stay here and rest today. Phoebe and Joel are taking care of your shop, and Agatha is tending to your home. Mary and Eb are taking care of chores."

"But Marcus…"

"I have just come back from the jail. Arsene is there now, and he intends to stay at Marcus's side until Takis orders him released. Your cousin is safe." Luke swallowed hard and took Lydia's hand. "It seems that Calchas intends to keep him in jail for as long as the law permits. He refuses to provide Takis any amount for compensation."

"This is his revenge on me," she said. "He is torturing Marcus. He knows I treasure my cousin above everyone in the world."

Luke nodded. "I believe you are right. Calchas strikes me that way as well." He drew a deep breath and expelled it slowly. "He cannot delay forever, though. If Calchas stalls too long, Marcus can appeal to a higher court. That would be dangerous for Takis, especially considering what happened with Paul and Silas. I think Takis will push him for a decision soon."

"Whatever Takis demands, I will pay," Lydia said, still wincing with her headache.

Luke smiled. "Do not worry about that now. Rest a bit longer. Your friends Syntyche and Euodia plan to come to see you for a little while. They want to pray for you."

"There is too much to do before the meeting tonight," Lydia said. "Agatha and the children cannot do everything."

Luke gave Lydia a scolding look. "You worry too much. You must sleep a little more. There will not be a large meeting tonight. The church will meet again in a few days. Until then, just a few will come to pray."

"But I should not be the cause..."

"Sleep, Lydia. In a few hours, your friends will be here. Then you can see what you are the cause of." Luke went to the window and closed the shutter to darken the room. "I will send Agatha to get you up when it is time."

Lydia tried to resist, but she felt the tug of sleep at her eyes. She began to breathe more slowly, and her aches ebbed away.

Two hours later, Lydia felt a warm hand covering hers.

She was not sure if she was awake or asleep, but she could hear voices.

"Lord, bless our dear friend and touch her with Your healing hand."

Lydia recognized the round, honey-toned voice as Euodia's. She smiled as she thought of her friends around her.

"We need Lydia to return to her gentle work in our city," Syntyche added. "Lord Jehovah, pour out Your mercy on her."

Lydia tried to open her eyes, but her eyelids felt stuck with too much sleep. She continued to listen to her friends.

Agatha's voice joined the others. "God and Father, hold Your child in Your grace," she said. Lydia noticed that Agatha sounded raspy as if she had been crying.

Another woman prayed, and then another, and another. Phoebe, Korinna, and Mary, Lydia thought. Her heart swelled at the tenderness that surrounded her bed.

Lastly, a voice that sounded like a wild breeze in the trees began to pray. "Lord, in the perfect name of Jesus Christ, I ask that You heal this woman." Lydia did not recognize who spoke.

She opened her eyes to see Daphne at her side, smiling. At that second, all the women said, "Amen."

Lydia felt strengthened and sat up in her bed, and her friends all surrounded her with hugs and smiles.

"Oh, Mistress, you look much better," Agatha said through a visibly relieved expression.

Lydia took a deep breath and realized her pain was gone.

Her head felt clear, and her muscles did not ache. "I am," she said. "I am better."

She got to her feet and dressed quickly. Agatha helped her comb her hair and pull it back from her face.

"You should eat something," Korinna said.

"I prepared some bread and spiced cheeses with an olive dip. Come downstairs, and we can all eat," Phoebe said.

The women formed a cloud around Lydia as she came down the steps. Luke waited at the bottom step. "I see you are feeling better?"

Lydia nodded, but before she could answer, Daphne chirped, "God has healed her, just as you said."

He followed the women into the great hall and nodded at the food on the table. "Do not allow her to get too excited. She will be weak still."

As the women all agreed, Luke left them to fellowship.

"I must get my house in order," Lydia said as she dipped her bread in the olive sauce. "I do not know what Calchas will demand, but I know he will want a significant amount of money."

Euodia and Syntyche giggled like young girls. "Luke has not told you?" Euodia asked.

Lydia shook her head. "Told me what?"

"When we all heard about your cousin, we gathered another collection." Syntyche gestured to the courtyard. "After supper, we will take you to see. Everyone brought something to your booth today, and Joel collected it all and brought it home for you."

As Lydia listened to her friends, she found herself barely

breathing. All she could manage to do was blink. "What do you mean?"

Agatha grinned and squeezed her hand. "Dear sister, whatever Calchas requires, you will be able to pay."

"I cannot accept money and gifts from others. I have plenty," Lydia argued.

"You have given generously because you have plenty," Korinna said. "I know this very well. Whenever someone is in need, you answer. You bless this city every day with your gifts."

Syntyche nodded and sipped her watered wine. "Now you must allow others to bless you."

"But I have so much..." Lydia started but then paused.

Mary finished for her. "And you have done well with that. God is blessing you with more, and He will expect a great deal more from you." She glanced at her mother, who nodded her approval.

Lydia was not sure quite how to respond. As she looked around the table at the smiles on her friends' faces, she just shrugged.

"Finish eating, Mistress," Agatha said. "Tomorrow will bring its own trouble, and you will need your strength. We all will."

CHAPTER

SEVENTEEN

Takis stared at Lydia as she marched toward him, and Lydia met his glare with a steady gaze. Joel followed behind her, leaving just enough distance to assure Takis exactly who was in charge.

"I wish to pay whatever fines you have levied against my cousin," she said once in Takis' hearing.

Takis lowered his lids until his eyes appeared as two black slits on either side of his narrow, angular nose. "I have not yet received Calchas' request for compensation," he answered flatly.

"It has been a week," Lydia declared with just enough volume that others in the marketplace turned their attention to the conversation. "Can you not judge for yourself what is fair in this instance?"

Takis began to fidget in his chair. To make his tick less noticeable, he stood. When his shoulder still twitched, he started his typical pacing. Lydia only now began to understand how much his fear of Calchas controlled him.

She took a step closer and lowered her voice. "Do not allow one man to hold your dignity ransom. Calchas cannot hurt you."

Takis pressed his lips into a thin straight line and lowered his face to her ear. "But he can hurt you, Lydia. I do not want to see you crushed under his fist."

Lydia took a step back and held her chin up. "I serve a God who will work through me to battle against the hate inside that man."

Takis shrugged. "You have one god. He has many."

"My God carries the burden of all creation," she said. "His gods sit on a table."

Takis laughed for a second and then straightened his face. "Come back in one hour."

Lydia and Joel marched back to her booth, and Ercole nodded as she passed.

"You did well, Mistress," Joel said. He watched as Takis did his best to appear official as he strode across the forum to Calchas' booth. "He is going in to speak with Calchas now."

She nodded and went to work organizing and straightening her merchandise, trying not to listen through the wall to the conversation next door.

Joel welcomed a shopper inside and directed the woman toward Lydia.

"May I help you find something special?" Lydia asked, relieved to have someone to serve.

"Yes," the woman replied, looking around the booth. "I have a friend named Theda, and she told me that you sold some very fine linen. I see that she was correct." The woman picked up a small bottle of dye and held it into the sunlight. "Oh yes, this is just the right color."

"That is a unique color. It comes directly from my family in Tyre," Lydia explained. "I have some fabric of the same hue as well, if you are looking for less work."

The woman nodded. "I would love to see that, too," she said.

Lydia picked up the cloth and held it out for the woman to touch. "It is a tight weave. It will keep the color for years."

"Lovely," the woman said. "I will take it. Theda told me you understood quality."

"Is your friend the wife of Alexander?"

"Yes," the woman answered. "Do you know her well?"

Lydia nodded and gestured to Joel. "Yes, Alexander and Theda are related to my friend, Phoebe—this is her husband, Joel."

The woman eyed Joel and nodded. "Yes, I see." She turned to Lydia and nodded. "Theda told me about the purples you sold. She said that you dedicated your booth to serve the one God. Is this so?"

Lydia smiled sweetly and nodded. "I serve Jesus, the Messiah, and His Father, the God of Creation. I have given my whole life over to Him—all that I have and all that I do. So, yes, this booth and all of my merchandise serve Him too."

"Hmmph," the woman said with a shrug. She let the bottle of expensive dye drop to the ground. The glass vial shattered and the purple liquid spattered on everything around it. "What a shame," the woman said, tossing the fabric in her hand down onto the mess. "Perhaps your

Messiah should make himself useful and clean this up." The woman marched out of the booth and back into the crowd of shoppers.

Joel started to grab her arm to stop her, but Lydia shook her head. "Just let her go. We can pray for her after we clear away the stained merchandise."

"I will take care of this," Joel said, bending down to tackle the mess. "Such a waste. This fabric is ruined."

"Nonsense," Lydia said. "I will take it to Agatha and Korinna. They can embroider over and around the spots and create a beautiful design. The only thing destroyed was the bottle that held the dye."

Joel shook his head and sighed. "You just refuse to allow anyone to upset you."

Lydia went back to the front of the booth for a moment of sunlight. She let the light warm her cheeks and arms and whispered a prayer for the woman's bitterness. A few days ago she might have become angry, but since the women prayed over her, her heart felt shielded and secure.

"What happened?" she heard Ercole say. "Your peplos is spattered all around the hem."

She turned to face him and took a breath. "A bottle of dye fell and broke. That happens sometimes."

Ercole appeared sincerely sympathetic. Calchas clicked his tongue and said, "Sad when accidents happen. And that one will cost you a great deal, I suppose."

"We will manage, Calchas," Lydia assured him.

The heavy-set man sauntered in front of her booth and stopped in just the right place to cast his shadow over her.

"You will need to watch every piece of silver for a while, my friend."

His tone and expression twisted *my friend* into an ugly insult. "I just gave Takis the figures to satisfy what I require for compensation. I imagine that he will double that in fines for your cousin. I think Marcus will be in jail for quite a while."

As he walked away, the sunlight again flooded Lydia's face, causing her to squint. She retreated into her booth to tell Joel. "I need to speak with Takis again. Calchas gave him his figures."

"Give me a minute more, and I will go with you," he said.

She agreed. As she waited at the front entrance, Luke and Agatha approached.

"We brought you something to eat," Agatha said.

"Thank you." Lydia gestured for her to set the basket on the back table. "Takis may have all the fines figured. I am going to see him again." She looked back into the booth where Joel worked. "Agatha, please stay here with Joel, and I will take Luke with me."

"Yes, Mistress," Agatha said. She turned to see what Joel was doing. "Oh, no," she cried when she saw the spattered dye.

Lydia gestured for Luke to follow as she started across the forum.

"What was that about?" Luke asked.

Lydia grinned. "We had a dissatisfied customer drop a bottle of dye. Joel is cleaning it up now."

Luke pointed to the bottom of her dress. "Is that what caused the spots?"

Lydia nodded and laughed. "Do you like them?"

"What about the rest of your fabrics?"

She shook her head. "I will not worry about them. I have wonderful women who can embroider such lovely designs around the new patterns. I will probably make even more money than I would have otherwise."

Luke sighed. "The Lord often takes our mistakes and turns them into blessings. I know He has done this many times for me."

As they reached Takis' office, he came out to greet them. "I have your news, Lydia. I do not think you will be pleased. Calchas' demands are high."

"I gave him almost twice what he paid for Daphne. I expect he demands much more than that for Marcus." Lydia stared at Takis with a look of anxious expectation, but he remained quiet for several seconds.

"Quite," he finally spat out. "I have the formal bill of fines here," he said, passing a document from his assistant's hand to her.

Lydia looked at the <u>fines</u> and held the paper where Luke could see. "Calchas wants ten minas for reparations, and Takis wants another two <u>minas</u> for expenses and penalties."

Luke made a growling sound. "Twelve hundred drachmas. Almost four years' wages."

Lydia shook her head. "I expected fifteen hundred," she whispered in his ear. Lydia turned her attention to Takis. "May I pay you now?" she asked.

Takis blinked in dismay. "I will require full payment *before* I can release Marcus."

Luke nodded. "If Lydia pays the fines now, will Marcus be released immediately?"

Takis laughed but then seemed to realize that Luke was not joking. "You have twelve minas with you now?"

Lydia handed back the bill. "I have it in my booth. I will count it out and bring it to you right away. You should send someone to the jail to prepare Marcus. I will go and collect him when I leave you."

Lydia did not wait for a reply before departing for her shop. Luke dipped his chin toward Takis and turned to follow his friend.

When they reached the shop, Lydia went right to the chest of silver and began counting.

"You should eat something," Agatha said. She was setting out a small meal on a table at the back.

"I cannot leave Marcus in a cell any longer." Lydia counted out the money and tucked the small box under her arm. She put the leftover money into a leather pouch and handed it to Luke. "We should send this to Paul to help his travels."

Luke nodded and took the purse. "Take care of Marcus first."

CHAPTER

EIGHTEEN

Lydia and Agatha reached the top of the marble stairway leading down to the entry of the prison. Lydia noticed and pointed out the cracks in the stones where the recent earthquake had left its mark.

"Such a dreary place," Agatha said. "I am sure Marcus will be glad to see you today."

Lydia took a deep breath and shrugged. She felt happy to have the wall beside the steps to steady herself. Her hands were trembling, and her heart pounded fast. "I hope he will. Every day I have come to see him and to show him my support. He has been polite but nothing more. He is an angry young man."

"Of course he is," Agatha said. "He was on a dangerous task for Calchas. He was beaten and robbed, and when he finally returned, Calchas had him beaten again."

Lydia nodded and took Agatha's hand as they reached the last step.

"Good afternoon," Arsene hailed them. "Marcus is almost ready to go with you. He is putting on the fresh tunic you sent him last night."

Lydia smiled. "Ercole brought his things back to my house this week. I will be glad to have him home again."

"Like the rest of your slaves?" Marcus said as he stepped out of jail and into the small yard. "Now you have purchased me, just like all the others?"

Lydia ran to his side to hold him, but Marcus held up his hands to halt her.

"Do not pretend in front of your friends, Lydia," Marcus said with a sneer.

"I do not understand," she replied. A rush of fear, sadness, and anger stirred her heart which had been strong only minutes before. Tears burned in her eyes, but she refused to let them fall. "I am here because I love you. I know you were jailed on false charges."

"Because if the charges were true, then you would be humiliated in this city?" Marcus spat back at her.

"No," she said. Her anger pushed her another step forward. "Even if you had stolen Calchas' money, I would still be here. I told you before: there is nothing you can do to diminish my love for you."

"I remember your words. But that is all they were."

"How can you speak to Lydia like that?" Agatha scolded. "She just paid a fortune for your freedom. She loves you like a mother."

"But she is not my mother!" Marcus said, and then raced up the steps and away from the others.

Lydia clasped her hands over her heart and started up

the stairs to try to catch him. Arsene and Agatha tried to stop her, but she ran almost as swiftly as Marcus.

As she reached the top step, Lydia saw him racing toward the Hellenic temple several yards away. She took a deep breath and chased after him. Lydia did not care that it was unseemly for women to run in public. All she knew was that she had to get to Marcus.

He was out of her sight by the time she reached the first columns at the temple entrance. A priestess stopped her. "Whom do you seek here?"

Lydia paused, trying to catch her breath. "A young man just ran past here. Did he go inside?"

The other woman spoke slowly as she glanced around. "No one has entered here for a little while. I saw someone pass a moment ago. I cannot say if it was a young man or old. He followed the road that direction." She pointed to the north. "Perhaps he went to one of those houses."

Lydia looked around but saw no one else. She could not see Marcus anywhere. As she looked down the road, she realized that Ercole's house was just a short distance away.

"Thank you," Lydia said. The woman nodded and retreated into the temple.

Lydia hurried in the direction the woman showed her, though she no longer ran. She was afraid she might miss Marcus in her rush. She approached Ercole's house, went to the door, and knocked. His young house servant answered the door.

"Yes, Mistress?"

"Can you tell me if Marcus is here?" Lydia asked. She scanned the hall behind the boy but could see no one.

"I am sorry, but Marcus's belongings were moved away this week. He does not live here anymore." The boy added an apologetic bow.

"I know that, but I thought I he might have come to see Ercole," she said.

The boy stared at her as if he was not sure how to answer. Lydia called out, "Marcus, are you here? I just want to talk to you."

He shook his head. "No one is here. Ercole is in the forum today, working. Perhaps you could speak to him."

Lydia shook her head and walked away. She did not know if this boy was hiding Marcus or if he was telling the truth. She looked up and down the road but saw nothing. Her cousin was just gone.

She began muttering to herself, but her frustrations clouded her mind and made her search impossible. As she walked back to the forum, she heard music rising from the Hellenic shrine. She recognized the song as one her mother had taught her as a child—a cry to Hera. The memory tore at her heart, and she scrambled for something to blot out the pagan words.

She began singing a psalm to herself. As she meditated on the picture her song painted about a tree growing at a river's edge, flourishing through a constant supply of water and sunlight, she began to feel calm and focused. The song from the temple faded.

Agatha and Luke waited for her in the center of the forum.

"Did you see where he went?" Agatha asked.

Lydia shook her head. "No. I went to Ercole's home, but he was not there."

Luke led the women back to Lydia's shop so she could rest. As they went inside, he gestured to the sky. "It looks like another storm is heading this way. You should go home soon. The market is all but empty now."

Lydia allowed her tears to escape. "He will not go home."

Luke shook his head. "You cannot know that. He does not have another place to go. Perhaps the storm will drive him home."

Lydia and Agatha exchanged a dubious glance. "We can close up," Lydia said. "But I think I will go to the palaestra before I go home. He has friends there."

Luke helped put the awnings down and secured the booth as the sky darkened above. "You and Agatha should go home," he told Joel. "I will go with Lydia to talk to Marcus's friends."

"I will," he replied. "Shall I send out word to the church?"

Luke nodded. "Yes, gather all the men to the house. Tell the women to stay in their homes and pray."

Joel and Agatha nodded and headed toward Alexander's booth. Luke and Lydia made their way around the agora to the south side of the palaestra field. Epaphroditus was standing with a group of friends and hailed them as they approached.

"Good day to you both," he said. "I was told that Marcus is free. I thank the Lord for you, Lydia."

Lydia kissed the young man's cheeks. "He is free, but he has run away from me, Epaphroditus. Have you seen him?"

The young man took several steps away from his wrestling friends to speak more privately with Lydia and Luke. "I have not seen him, but I will be happy to look for him. Some of the others here have had harsh words for Marcus. Calchas has been spreading rumors all over the city. I fear what might happen to him if the wrong person finds him."

Lydia frowned and wrung her hands in worry, and as soon as she became aware of it, she forced herself to stop. "Thank you for caring about him. You are a good friend."

Luke nodded. "Can you talk to Ercole, too? Lydia went to his house earlier, but Marcus was not there. Ercole might not talk to either of us if he thinks Calchas will find out."

"I will." Epaphroditus nodded. "If I find Marcus, I will either take him to your home or mine."

"That will be fine," Lydia said. She kissed his cheek again. "When you have exhausted your search, please come to my house, and we will feed you."

Epaphroditus laughed. "When I am done searching, I will have Marcus at my side."

Luke gripped the young man's wrist. "You are a good man."

CHAPTER

NINETEEN

The storm started as a light rain but within an hour became a deluge. By the time the first group of men went out to search, there was standing water in Lydia's courtyard, and lightning flashed around the peak of Mount Orbelos. Thunder echoed from one mountain to another rolling around the valley.

Lydia stood at her front door in the meager protection of her portico. Her clothes were soaked with rain, but she refused to go into the house. At his mother's instruction, Eb brought her a dry blanket for warmth. "Please come inside, Mistress," he urged.

"Soon," she said. "Soon Marcus will be home."

Mary, Phoebe, and Daphne took turns waiting with her in the rain. Agatha brought her a bowl of stew, and Lydia ate a few bites before sending the rest back. "I cannot eat."

Agatha shook her head and clucked. "Luke will be cross with me if I allow you to catch a fever again."

"Luke understands," Lydia said, as Agatha went back inside.

Korinna sat just inside the door, sewing and singing. Phoebe had been teaching her several lullabies. Her sweet voice gave Lydia a thread of calm to hold in her otherwise racing thoughts.

After hours of pacing, Lydia finally succumbed to her exhaustion and sat on the cold marble floor. Daphne came running to her side. "Are you all right?" she asked.

Lydia nodded and clasped the young girl's hands tightly. "Lord, I thank You for bringing this child to Philippi. You have brought a blessing to my home through her, and I praise You."

Daphne leaned in and rested her head on Lydia's shoulder. "Thank You, God, most high," the child whispered.

"Lord of creation, I praise Your holy name and beg for your mercy," Lydia continued. "Please deliver Marcus back to our home and show us how to reach him with Your never-ending love and patience." Her tears flowed and mingled with the raindrops that raced over her face. "Please, Lord Jehovah, please bring him back to me."

A stirring in the darkness caught Lydia's attention, and when she looked up, Daphne turned to see it, too.

A group of men appeared beyond the trees and hurried through the storm to her front steps. The lanterns on the portico were weak, and Lydia jumped to her feet to see if Marcus was with them. Luke led the men up the steps, with Alexander and Joel close behind and on either side of young Gallus, carrying him.

"Where is Marcus? Did you find him?" she asked.

Luke shook his head. "Not yet. The storm is fierce. Gallus fell and hurt his leg." He directed the other men carrying the young man. "Take him inside and get him dry and warm. Make him something hot to drink, so he is warmed on the inside, too. Clean his wound, and I will attend him."

Alexander nodded, and everyone went in the house except Lydia and Luke.

"You should come in out of the rain, too. You will be sick if..." he began.

"Marcus is out in this, and he has no shelter!" Lydia cried. She gulped in a breath of air mixed with tears and rain and began to cough.

"You want to see him come home," Luke said, taking her arms gently in his hands. "You must take care. I have seen many people succumb to vicious fevers that arise from the combination of hunger, fatigue, heartache, and cold rain. You must see to yourself."

Lydia shook her head and tried to push out of Luke's arms. "You do not understand. He is all I have." Her voice cracked under the strain of sobs.

Luke pulled her closer and held her against his chest. "No, Lydia. Marcus is not all you have. You have a whole host of people who love you. Marcus knows that he can come home. He knows that you love him. The choice is his now."

Lydia finally pulled free and took several steps away from him. She braced her shivering body against the cold marble column at the entry. "Go inside and take care of Gallus. I will search for Marcus myself." She turned to the wall hook that held her lantern and struggled to release it so that she could carry it with her into the blackness beyond her steps. Luke took hold of her hands, but she pushed him away. "Let me go."

"Then let me help you get the lamp down," he said. Lydia turned to face the storm, refusing to look him in the eye. As he handed her the dimming light, he said, "Wait here, and I will bring you a cloak."

She nodded and waited as he went into the house. All she could think about was Marcus as a small child. The day his mother died, he had run out into the olive grove to hide when a storm came up. She and Simeon searched for hours to find him and bring him home. She did not know where Marcus was, but she knew he was not hiding in the trees this time.

She stood and stared into the night, wishing he would walk through the clearing and into her arms. She could not see him anywhere. She could not see the trees. She could not see the clearing. The blackness of the storm was like a curtain, interrupted only by occasional flashes of lightning.

She held the lantern up and strained to focus on something moving just a few yards away. She could only hear rain and fading thunder. She could see only shadows and flickers of light in the rain.

"Please, Lydia," Luke said as he draped a cloak around her shoulders. "If you can wait for just a little longer, I will go with you. I just need to..."

Whatever Lydia was seeing, Luke saw it too. He grabbed the lantern from her and stepped back into the gale. "Is someone there?" he called out.

Two men stumbled out of the grove on the path to Lydia's house. One fell face down into the mud, and the other struggled to lift him back to his feet. Luke raced to help them.

"Lydia, help," Luke shouted. "He found him."

She rushed down the steps to the men. Epaphroditus stumbled under the weight of Marcus's half-conscious body. Luke handed the lamp back to Lydia and scooped Marcus up. He carried him into the main hall of the house.

Epaphroditus and Luke settled Marcus onto a couch. "Wrap him in a warm blanket," Luke said. "Did he walk on his own, or did you carry him the whole way?" he asked Epaphroditus.

Epaphroditus shook with drenched chills. "Ercole and I searched everywhere. He found him behind the Hellenic temple, screaming to himself. Ercole helped me carry him to the edge of the tree line. He did not want to come farther."

Lydia nodded and patted Epaphroditus' shoulder. "Go get something to eat. Ask Eb for something dry to wear."

"I would rather stay here with Marcus," he replied.

Luke shook his head. "Take care of yourself first. Do it quickly and come right back. I will need your assistance."

Epaphroditus left with Eb, anxious to get back and help. Luke shot a stern glance at Lydia. "You should dry yourself, too. I need your hands warm and steady."

"I am fine."

"Do as I tell you, Lydia. Marcus is in desperate shape. Go. Right now." Luke glared at her until she conceded.

Lydia hated to leave her cousin, but she could not deny the trembling that had overtaken her body. She raced upstairs and changed into a fresh linen peplos. She combed her thick curls, squeezing the rainwater into the basin on her dressing table. She took a small thin shawl and wrapped her hair tightly in it, twisting it around her head and securing the end with a small brass pin. Already she felt warmer.

When she rushed back to the main hall, Agatha had a cup of broth for her to sip. In her hurry, she gulped it down and scalded her tongue. Her thoughts darted about trying to think of what to say and do to bring Marcus back to health.

Luke finished wrapping bandages around Gallus' injury just as Joel and Alexander replaced the blanket covering Marcus with a fresh one, warmed by the fire.

Marcus's face glistened with sweat, and Lydia could feel the heat radiating from his head and neck. She reached for his hand, which was cold and clammy. "What is wrong?" she asked Luke. "His head is hot, and his hands are cold."

Luke's expression looked grave. His voice was low and serious. "His blood is slow, thick with infection. Phoebe is making a poultice, but we must pray that it works. Epaphroditus told me that he drank a lot of wine mixed with spices and herbs. He is not well at all."

Lydia stared at Marcus and cried. His skin looked pale, almost transparent. The sagging flesh around his eyes was dark and sunken. His lips looked blue and thin, so different from the hearty, tanned smile she loved.

Luke pulled Marcus's arms from beneath the blanket and began massaging the muscles, starting at the shoulder and working down to the wrist. "Do as I do, Lydia. Rub hard, too."

She followed his example and began kneading her

cousin's arm. As she did, she watched Luke's expression grow more and more concerned. He looked determined, but also fearful.

"What else can we do?" she asked.

Just then Phoebe brought in a bowl of crushed ingredients with a strange smell of onions and dates. Mary followed with an armful of bandages.

Luke pulled the blanket back from Marcus's torso and began to spread the poultice mix over his chest. "Help me raise him," he instructed Lydia.

Lydia and Epaphroditus lifted Marcus forward while Luke wrapped the strips of linen loosely around him. When he was finished, they lowered him back into place and pulled the blanket back to his chin.

"Now we wait," Luke said. He got up and took a deep breath. "I will go and wash my hands, and then I will come back to pray over him."

Lydia could control her emotions no longer. A flood of tears covered her face, and she stretched her arms over Marcus and rested her head against his chest. She had sobbed for several seconds before she realized that she could hear a slow, faint heartbeat. She listened. The sound seemed to slow and grow weaker. She could barely hear Marcus breathing at all. She lifted her head from his torso, hoping to ease the weight on his lungs.

As she watched his chest rise and fall, she could see his ability to breathe fading. Her mind raced. She tried to pray, but words failed her. She wrestled with her thoughts and emotions. For a moment, only regret filled her mind, and another wave of tears fell. *I am going to lose him,* she thought.

Will my God answer a prayer for someone who does not believe? Should I petition Marcus's gods to save him? What can any god do for him? What can I do?

"Lydia, where is your heart?"

Lydia looked up, half-expecting to see Simeon in front of her. Instead, it was Luke. He stared at her, studying her face. Lydia knew her doubt showed to everyone in the room. She felt ashamed.

"What can I do to save him?" Lydia held up her hands in surrender. "Can anyone save him?"

Luke tilted his head. "There is nothing you can do to save him. That is not your place. Only Jesus can save anyone. It is only through Him that we can be with God. You must turn Marcus over to Jesus."

She listened with an aching heart. She wanted Marcus to come to know Jesus, and she had let her fears and worries get in the way. All she had shown Marcus was anxiety and busyness. Lydia wore them like the pearl powder across her face, now streaked with dirt and tears. She never let the peace of God shine through to the one for whom she cared most, and now she might never have another chance.

"I am lost," she confessed.

Luke took her hands and shook his head. "You are in a valley of desolation, but you are not lost."

Everyone in the house came into the front hall and surrounded Lydia, Marcus, and Luke. One at a time, Agatha, Joel, Phoebe, Mary, Eb, Korinna, Daphne, Epaphroditus, Alexander, and Gallus came up to Marcus and formed a circle. They all joined Lydia and Luke in placing hands on

Marcus, wherever they could reach, and kept them there while they prayed together.

Luke began, and as he prayed the others joined in concordance. They asked for healing, blessing, and deliverance for Marcus and revelation for the whole household.

Lydia poured out her heart to God silently as the others prayed aloud. As she struggled to find the right words, she could almost hear a voice in her ear.

"Do not be afraid, child. I am with him. I have been with him all along. You have only to love him. That is all I ask of you, and it is more than enough."

"Yes, Lord," she responded. She felt Luke's hand over hers, and she felt something else. It was more than peace. It was more than comfort. It was a reassurance that her God had found her. It was a faith of her own.

As they finished the prayer with a layered "Amen," a blinding white light flashed, and a deafening crash of thunder shook the house. A fine mist of dust shook loose from the ceiling beams, smothering several of the lamps in the room. Darkness enveloped the group.

Young Mary gasped, and Korinna began to sing a lullaby with a tremble in her voice. Joel scrambled to relight the lantern on the wall, and when the little glow finally filled the crowded space, everyone saw what had happened. Marcus was sitting up, of his own strength, looking at Lydia.

"What happened?" he asked.

Lydia threw her arms around him and squeezed as if she might never let him go. "Oh, Marcus, you are back," she said.

Marcus's face was no longer ashen but plumped and pink. His eyes shone brightly as he blinked through an expression of bewilderment. "How did I get back here?" he asked.

Lydia sat upright and held his hand, gazing with wonder into his eyes and watching the color of life returning to his face. "Ercole and Epaphroditus carried you home."

Marcus took a deep breath, and as the blanket fell to his waist, he examined the bandages around his chest. "Where is the other man?"

Luke patted Marcus's arm. "Ercole did not want to stay. He is still afraid of Calchas and what he might do."

Marcus shook his head. "Not Ercole. The *other* man."

Lydia and Luke both turned toward Epaphroditus. He shrugged. "There was no one else but Ercole and me."

Marcus scratched the back of his neck. "There was a man in a white robe. I was cold and wet, but when he touched my forehead, I was warm and dry. He told me that I should listen to you." He pointed to Luke. "He said that you spoke the truth and that I should do exactly as you instruct."

Luke's eyes filled with tears and he grasped Marcus's wrist in his right hand.

Lydia was trembling with every word. "What does this mean?" she asked. "Who did he see?"

Marcus stared at Luke and smiled. "Do you have something to tell me?" he asked.

Luke began to laugh. "Yes, my brother. Praise be to God, I have a great many things to tell you."

Marcus reached for his cousin and pulled her to his side. He kissed Lydia's forehead and squeezed her hand. "The man told me how much you love me. He showed me a bowl of the most fragrant incense I have ever smelled. They were your prayers for me, he said. They were beautiful. I love you, too."

Lydia held his hand and squeezed, never wanting to let her cousin go.

Marcus turned his full attention to Luke. "When can you begin?"

"'All this time I have been calling you,' he told me," Marcus explained.

Ercole listened intently as the two young men sat in the sunshine of the courtyard. Lydia and Luke sat on the bench facing them.

"But there was no one else," Ercole said. "I was there. It was just Epaphroditus and you and me."

"He told me that my heart was strong and that I would be a messenger for Him." Marcus placed his hand firmly on his friend's shoulder. "His calling is something I can no longer refuse, Ercole. You know me. I have spent all this time searching for something greater than myself. Searching for my place."

Ercole nodded. "We have talked about this many times. You have always believed that you were meant to do great things. But how can you be sure that he is the highest god? Can one god manage the whole world?"

Marcus laughed. "The Roman pantheon of gods cannot even manage themselves. They are meager ideals of man."

Luke added, "Jehovah God is beyond time and mortal convention. He established absolutes."

"And Jesus of Nazareth is a lower god? I do not understand." Ercole sighed and glanced to Luke and Lydia. "I do not mean to be contrary. I just want to know."

Lydia smiled. "You are not the only follower of Jesus to notice this mystery. The best explanation I can offer goes like this: God, the Father, is in heaven. Jesus, the Son, gave up his throne for a while to come to earth to share with us the Holy Spirit, which is also a part of God. The mystery of how God could walk the earth as a man and still be God is essential in the Christian faith. But God as Father, God as Son, and God as Holy Presence working through us are not separate things. Together they are God. There is no lower god. Someday a wiser person may explain it better, but this answer helps me and may help you."

"Ercole, do not be ashamed of seeking the truth," Marcus said. "All the time I was searching for power from the heavens, I was running from the truth. Jesus is not a lower god. He is God. The Father, Son, and Holy Spirit are one God in three forms. I know it is difficult to understand, but when you open your heart, the Lord pours out a measure of understanding."

Ercole nodded. "I can see the evidence in you, my friend. Your anger has drifted away like the storms over the mountains."

Marcus inhaled a deep breath and released it slowly. "It

is not my doing. It is the Spirit within me. I have a purpose now. I have a message to share."

Ercole looked at the ground. "I have only chores to do and sacrifices to make." He twitched his shoulders. "If I forget what to do, Calchas is more than happy to remind me —usually at the top of his voice."

Marcus took his friend's wrist. "Following Jesus only requires one sacrifice. You must give up everything. Your whole life. But it is not so difficult when you see what He has given up for you, and what He offers in return."

Ercole chewed on his lip. "Calchas will be furious with me. He will no longer have an assistant to order around. I could never go back to working in his booth."

Lydia glanced at Luke with an expression of hope. She knew Ercole's heart was turning.

Marcus shrugged. "We will pray that Calchas will hear and accept the good news of Jesus as well."

Ercole chuckled. "I think it would take a miracle for Calchas to believe in anything but Calchas."

Lydia made a quick gesture to catch the younger men's attention. "Ercole, I must confess something to you now. When I first committed my life to Jesus, I prayed for days that you and Calchas would fold up your business and move away from Philippi. At the time, I believed that you both were out of my God's reach." She dipped her chin. "Jesus is stronger than anything I could have imagined."

Luke squeezed her hand. "He still amazes me every day with the way He works his will through other people."

"I suppose if Jesus can turn my heart around, then He can use anyone for His good work," Marcus said with a laugh. "If

I had listened to Lydia right from the beginning then I would have saved everyone lots of trouble."

Luke shook his head. "Perhaps, but that would have deprived the rest of us of a valuable lesson to learn. Besides, look at what the Lord is doing with you now. You have a very clear idea about how much Jesus loves you. You have dipped your toes into the pool of death that comes with the pursuit of idols. You have recast your life and changed your future."

Marcus grimaced. "The pool of death. How apt. But I have indeed found that the cleansing waters of life are better, and I want everyone to know that."

Ercole sighed and pressed the palms of his hands against his eyes. "How much more must I learn before Luke can baptize me? How soon can I leave this present hell where I am stranded?" he asked.

Lydia closed her eyes and offered a quick prayer of thanksgiving. Luke stood and reached out to take Ercole's wrist. "There are no tasks to complete. No lessons or tests to take. There is no way to earn your salvation. There is only faith and obedience."

Ercole stood and nodded. "Well, I do believe that Jesus is the Son of God. I have seen His hand over this city and in the hearts of my friends. I am eager to see what He can do with a sinner like me."

Marcus stood beside his friend and embraced him. "I have learned that it can be a joyful partnership, and He will work through you in ways you could never predict."

Luke nodded in agreement, and Lydia reached out for Ercole's face. She stood up on her toes to kiss his cheeks. "I am glad I was wrong about you. This turn in you has taught me to pray for Calchas in a different way. I shall not give up on him."

Luke and Marcus took Ercole to the stable and baptized him together while Lydia sang a psalm of praise and joy.

As soon as Ercole was out of the water, he exclaimed, "I must go and tell Calchas what I have done. I am not afraid of what he can do to me anymore."

Marcus kissed Lydia and Luke on the cheeks. "I will go with him. We can tell Epaphroditus and Gallus on the way."

The young men's excitement gave Lydia a thrill as she watched them disappear into the olive grove.

She held her hands over her heart and, without a second thought, leaned back against Luke's chest.

He put his arms around her and whispered into her ear. "This is a good day."

She turned to face him, still within his arms. She put her hands on either side of his face and kissed his cheeks. "Thank you, Luke. You have brought life back into my house."

He held her face in his hands and returned the kisses on her cheeks. "You have given me a home here in Philippi, but you have done much more. Watching you employ your faith with the problems of your home and city have strengthened my own faith. And while it is true that I love you in the Christian sense of the word, it is also true that I love you in another way. In the way that a man loves a woman. I do not want to frighten you or cause you to suspect that my motives are not entirely about spreading the word of Jesus, but I owe you the truth. I cannot help but love you."

"I have a similar feeling for you, Luke." She rested her

head on his shoulder. "I have great respect and admiration for what you do in the world as a healer and as a follower of Christ, but I am also aware of your qualities as a man. To be equally honest with you, I did not expect to feel like this again."

Luke wrapped his arms around her shoulders and pulled her more tightly. "I did not want to stir this feeling. Not within you or me. I failed." He sighed. "There are always complications."

Lydia nodded. She knew exactly what he meant. In her heart, she wanted nothing more than to spend her life at Luke's side. However, her mind told her that he had work to do in other places. *I could go with him*, she thought. *But you know that you have a calling of your own.* She buried her face in his chest.

"What is wrong?" Luke asked, holding her head in his hand. The tone of his voice told Lydia that he already knew. Without looking into his eyes, she moved so that her forehead rested against his jaw.

"You will leave us one day, and I will not be able to go with you," she said. A lump swelled in her throat, making it difficult for her to speak.

He did not respond with words, but she could feel his tears on her face. She could hold back the flood of sobs no longer. They stood and cried together for several minutes. Their emotions of sadness and joy mingled with their tears.

Finally, Luke took a step back and began dabbing at the damp streaks on Lydia's face. "We are together right now, walking in the same direction. We are dear friends, bound together by our Lord. We shall continue to walk together on the path set before us, and we will listen for God's perfect instruction. If we listen to Him, we can follow where he leads."

Lydia nodded, swallowing hard. She did not want to let Luke go, but she had faith that God would use her to do His will in His time.

Luke kissed her again. "We shall see what His plan holds for us both."

TWENTY-ONE

"And the Lord extended His hand to her and asked, 'Where have your accusers gone?'" Luke said. "The men had all left. They knew their test had failed."

"And then what did Jesus tell her?" Lydia asked. Listening to Luke's stories about Jesus, she could almost see them playing out in her mind.

"He told her to go home and leave her sins behind."

Lydia nodded. "He shows such kindness and compassion."

Luke tilted his head. "The woman went back and told everyone how He had forgiven her..."

"Help! Help!" A scream grew louder through the trees.

Lydia and Luke hopped to their feet and ran to Epaphroditus as he raced through the grove to Lydia's house.

"What is it?" she asked.

"Ercole is badly hurt," he said. "Luke, you must come quickly."

Luke rushed back into the house for his bag and returned within seconds.

"What happened to Ercole?" Lydia asked.

Epaphroditus wheezed as he spoke, leading them to the forum as quickly as he could manage.

"Calchas went mad and began beating him with one of his brass idols. Marcus tried to stop him, but Calchas would not relent. Takis' soldiers had to step in to get the situation under control." Epaphroditus pointed to Lydia's booth as they all reached the agora. "Ercole and Marcus are in your shop."

Lydia and Luke sped through the shoppers and into the booth of purple. Marcus hovered over his friend in the back of the shop. Ercole lay on the ground, covered in blood. His head was cut and bruised, and his tunic was ripped away, exposing deep gashes around his neck and shoulders.

Marcus cried out in prayer, "Lord, save him. Lord Jesus, save him."

Luke dropped to his knees at Marcus's side, noticing that Marcus had a slice through his upper arm, too. "I will take care of Ercole, but you need to let Lydia look after your arm."

"Heal him, Jesus. God, as you healed me, heal Ercole," Marcus continued to moan.

Lydia pulled her cousin away from Luke and helped him up to the bench against the side of the booth. "Let me wrap your wound," she said.

As she tended Marcus's injury, she watched Luke work on Ercole.

"This will hurt a little," Luke told him. "Try to keep your eyes open."

Lydia heard Ercole scream as Luke poured something over his cuts.

"I know," Luke tried to console him.

"Calchas flew into a rage, Lydia," Marcus said. "He would have killed Ercole. He would have killed me. His eyes blazed with fire."

Lydia realized she was holding her breath. "Thank God you are safe."

Marcus nodded. "Takis' soldiers came and pulled him away. Calchas struck one of them, too. They carried Calchas right to the jail."

"He will not be released for a long time," Takis said, his voice landed heavy behind them.

They all turned to see him standing in the doorway of the shop.

Marcus eyed the magistrate and nodded. "Thank you for rescuing us from Calchas' wrath."

"It is my duty to Philippi to protect every citizen," Takis replied. "It is evident to me now that Calchas is not the man of moderation and respect that he proclaims to be."

Lydia shook her head and swallowed back her fear. "Do you need Marcus to speak in the forum?"

"That will not be necessary," Takis answered. "Calchas made a spectacle of himself in public. I have more than enough charges against him. I have come to see if a charge of murder will be added."

Lydia and Marcus turned quickly toward Luke and Ercole. "How bad is it?" Marcus asked.

Luke looked over his shoulder for a moment and frowned. "Ercole's injuries are severe."

"Send word to me when you know something definite," Takis said. He crossed his arms over his chest and walked back to his office.

Lydia and Marcus moved to either side of Luke. Marcus held Ercole's head in his lap. "Come on, brother, hold on to my hand. You cannot leave us now."

Lydia whispered a prayer as she dabbed away the blood from Ercole's face. "Jehovah God, heal our friend. His faith is in You, and his body is in Your hands."

"The Lord has used me," Ercole said, struggling for breath. "The one true God shines His face upon me."

Lydia nodded and continued, "Elohai, my God, the soul You have breathed in us is pure. One day You will take it from us and restore it in the time to come. As long as it is within us, we will thank You."

Ercole smiled and turned his face toward Marcus. "You will never have to fear Calchas again. Philippi sees who he is now."

Luke moved swiftly to wrap bandages over each of Ercole's wounds. Marcus shook his head. "Do not leave us, Ercole. We need you."

"Do not be angry with God," Ercole whispered. "He has not left me, Marcus. His power does not diminish if I die. His kingdom increases as I go to be with him. I praise the one true God."

Lydia and Marcus wept and prayed while Luke did his best to care for Ercole. Suddenly a song rose from the front of the shop as several members of the church gathered.

"His love endures forever," the group sang, their hands clasped together to form one body. A short piece of purple cording encircled the wrists of each person gathered. "We will serve in the house of the Lord for all of our days."

"Amen," Ercole said before he lost consciousness.

TWENTY-TWO

Six years later...

"They are coming! They are coming!" little Matthew squealed as he ran inside from the olive grove. "Mother, Father, they are almost here."

Marcus and Korinna went to the portico to greet Daphne and Epaphroditus. The rest of the house buzzed with excitement as the young couple returned to the place where they first met. Korinna shifted her infant daughter to rest on her hip to kiss her dear friends and welcome them inside.

"Come in from the sun," she said. "We have everything ready."

Daphne quickly snatched the baby from Korinna, and Epaphroditus swung Matthew over his back and carried him to the table.

"It is a blessing to be back here," Epaphroditus said. "Now that our wedding month is ended, we will spend more time with our brothers and sisters."

"Where is Lydia?" Daphne asked. "I want to see her before everything becomes too busy. And Luke as well."

"I am here," Lydia called from the top of the stairs. She looked at her children with a mixture of love and sadness. As she descended the steps, she felt her heart wrestling within her. "This is difficult to see you all together again, no matter how wonderful it may be. It means my time with you is growing short."

She hugged and kissed her family, one precious soul at a time, hoping to prolong every second with them.

Daphne blinked back tears as she held Lydia's hand. "When will you be leaving?" Daphne asked.

"The church will be arriving soon for worship, we will celebrate communion, and then we will be going after that," Lydia explained. "Everything is packed for the journey, and Agatha and Joel have already taken our things to the docks. Marcus and Ercole will see us off at Neapolis. After taking us to the ship, they will return to the forum to open the booth."

"I wish we could see you to your ship, too," Daphne said.

"No, dear one," Lydia said, feeling her heart breaking. "I cannot bear it. I want to leave you here in a celebration. Too many tears if you all came to the ship. You all must carry on without us for a little while."

"You have been my mother," Daphne said. Her voice trembled and squeaked. "The only mother I have ever known. How can I carry on?"

Lydia placed one hand on Daphne's head and one on baby Chloe's back. "You have been the very best daughter any mother could hope to have." She kissed her again. "You are strong in the Lord. You will be fine without me. And do not worry, child. I will be back if it is the Lord's will. He has called me to take his message to my family in Thyatira, and I am happy to go."

Daphne nodded and forced a smile. "Is it not too dangerous to travel alone?"

Lydia patted her knee. "Luke and I will go together to Troas, and my brother will meet me there. If it is the Lord's will, Luke will join me back here later. Or perhaps I will join him. I will never be alone, though. You and I both know that."

Korinna sat down beside the women and placed a new scarf around Lydia's shoulders. She had embroidered the pale blue linen with dark purple scrollwork and flowers. Korinna smiled. "It is just a token to remind you of the house in which you serve."

"How lovely," Lydia said, caressing the buttery fabric between her fingers. "Thank you."

"What will the church do without either of you?" Korinna asked.

Lydia shook her head. "You will flourish. Luke could not stay here forever. We knew this from the beginning. He has been training leaders for years, and now it is time for them to lead. Paul wrote to Luke—he needs him at his side again, and Luke is eager to go to him."

Marcus and Epaphroditus joined the women's conversation. "It is more dangerous for Christians now," Marcus said. "There are many dying for their faith all over the Empire. Those of us who know the truth must stand up for what we believe. We must set an example for those whose faith is weak."

Epaphroditus stood up as Luke and Ercole entered from the courtyard. "Luke, brother, it is good to see you again." He clasped wrists with both men. "Ercole, you look well."

Luke and Ercole both greeted the others with a kiss on each cheek. "Everything is ready for our morning of praise with you all," Luke said. He went to Lydia's side and wrapped his arm around her shoulder. "My dear Rachel, let us pray together once more before our brothers and sisters arrive."

Luke surveyed the faces of his beloved friends. "Do not look sad, family," he said. "We will see each other again, in this world or in the next. We can be certain of that. God has promised us all a place in His kingdom, and God always keeps His promises."

"Amen," Daphne whispered, still fighting tears.

Her new husband cinched her close to his side. "Amen," Epaphroditus added with a nod.

Soon everyone joined together with a louder, more confident, "Amen!"

Lydia's heart soared with pride as she looked around the room. Marcus and Korinna held their precious children in their arms. Daphne and Epaphroditus shared a smile that warmed her heart. Ercole's strength and faith anchored the whole gathering. Luke's love and devotion to serving the Lord encouraged her to reach out to others wherever He might send her.

She longed to take the good news of Jesus to her family back in Thyatira. After so many years, she now had the opportunity to do it. *Lord God, You gave this to me*, she thought. She squeezed Luke's steady hand. *You gave this to me.*

As they held each other close and praised their God together, Lydia felt a stirring in her heart that she knew she would take with her for the rest of her life.

THE END

About the Author

Kimberly Black is an award-winning author, designer, Bible school teacher, and speaker. She lives in the Texas Panhandle with her husband, children, and fur-babies.
She enjoys writing historical Christian fiction, children's books, sci-fi, suspense, short stories, and her blog.
Please visit her website for more information.
www.kimblackink.com

More Books by Kimberly Black

Lydia, Woman of Purple, Devotional Study Guide
Her Most Precious Gift
Her Most Precious Gift, Devotional Study Guide
Pockets (children's book)
Sophie Louise Will Not Say CHEESE (children's book)